Because their parents have gone to Paris for a week and their usual sitter is not feeling well, Melissa, Amanda, and Pee Wee are being taken care of by their father's sister from Canada. It turns out that Aunt Sally is full of fascinating stories all about her and their father growing up on Vancouver Island. Pee Wee, Amanda, and Melissa are kept in thrall by the eccentric characters Aunt Sally brings to life, particularly the trolls, who changed Aunt Sally's family forever . . .

Polly Horvath has produced a small gem. She knows just how to twist language to make readers sit up and take notice and she draws her characters with such precision that they peak without ever going over the top . . . For those willing to look more closely, Horvath sneaks in a message about the ways sisters and brothers trick and treat one another, and how the family bond is as fragile as its most sensitive member. —*The New York Times Book Review*

★[Aunt Sally's] tales, like true family stories, vary in tone, exaggeration, and completeness, but they wield their power through their ability to relate the past to the present. Each story is entertaining on its own, and together they define the tone of this witty, clever, and involving book.

—STARRED / *Booklist*

It would be enough that *The Trolls* is very funny. It is splendid that it is more than merely enough.

—*The Bulletin of the Center for Children's Books*

THE TROLLS

POLLY HORVATH

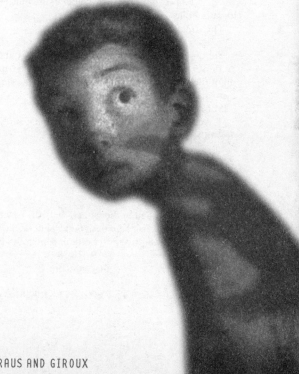

SQUARE
FISH

FARRAR, STRAUS AND GIROUX

**SQUARE
FISH**

An Imprint of Macmillan

Library of Congress Cataloging-in-Publication Data
Horvath, Polly.
    The trolls / Polly Horvath.
        p. cm.
    Summary: Eccentric Aunt Sally comes from Canada to babysit the
Anderson children while their parents are on a trip to Paris and every
night the bedtime story adds another piece to a very suspect family
history.
    ISBN 978-0-312-38419-7
    [1. Aunts—Fiction.   2. Trolls—Fiction.   3. Family Life—Fiction.
4. Brothers and sisters—Fiction.]   I. Title.

PZ7.H79224Tr   1999
[E]—dc21

                                                                98-3437

Originally published in the United States by Farrar Straus Giroux
Square Fish logo designed by Filomena Tuosto
First Square Fish Edition: September 2008
7 9 10 8 6
mackids.com

AR: 5.4 / F&P: S / LEXILE: 810L

For Lesley
• • •

Contents

THE
TROLLS

AUNT SALLY ARRIVES!

The week before Mr. and Mrs. Anderson were to leave Tenderly, Ohio, for the somewhat more bustling metropolis of Paris, their babysitter, who had just returned from far-off climes herself, came down with a mild case of bubonic plague and called tearfully to say she didn't want to spread the buboes around.

"Oh dear, take care of yourself," said Mrs. Anderson. "And don't worry, I'm sure we can find someone."

"Well, call me if you really get stuck," said the babysitter.

"I'm sure we won't," said Mrs. Anderson hastily and hung up. She wrung her hands and told Mr. Anderson the bad news. He immediately began phoning everyone he could think of. No one was available. Even the babysitting agencies were all booked up. Melissa Anderson, ten years old, Amanda Anderson, eight years old, and Pee Wee Anderson, six years old, watched their parents, Mr. and Mrs. Anderson, pace around the living room waving their nonrefundable tickets.

"Well, this is a fine kettle of fish," said Mrs. Anderson.

"What about a kennel?" said Pee Wee. "Are you going to put us in a kennel?"

"No," said Mr. Anderson, "we are not."

"Kennels are for dogs," said Melissa, who always knew everything.

"She said *kettle*," said Amanda, who often knew everything.

"Oh," said Pee Wee, who knew nothing and led the life of a worm.

Mr. and Mrs. Anderson told the children that they needed grownup time to work things out. They made Melissa, Amanda, and Pee Wee go to bed early, went into the living room, and shut the door. The Anderson children crept downstairs and peeked through the keyhole.

"What are they doing?" whispered Amanda to Melissa, who was kneeling in front of the door.

"Mom is pulling fluffies off her sweater," said Melissa.

"Oh dear," said Amanda.

"Dad is sweating," said Melissa.

"Oh dear," said Amanda.

"How can you see him sweating?" asked Pee Wee.

"I don't see it, I smell it," said Melissa. "I have a great nose."

"You would be happy in a kennel," said Pee Wee.

"I'm not going to a kennel," said Melissa.

"I thought we told you to drop that idea," said Amanda, looking sternly at Pee Wee.

"WAIT A SECOND!" the children heard Mrs. Anderson cry.

"Mom's jumping around," said Melissa.

"Let me look," said Amanda, shoving Melissa out of the way.

Mrs. Anderson was clasping her hands rhapsodically. "There's your sister!"

"She's going to be in Chicago, remember?" said Mr. Anderson glumly.

"No, not Lyla. *Sally!*" said Mrs. Anderson.

There was silence.

"What are they doing? Let *me!*" said Melissa, pushing Amanda away from the keyhole.

"No, let *me!*" said Pee Wee. He tried to push against Melissa, but she was rooted to the floor.

"Daddy looks stunned," said Melissa.

"Who's Sally?" asked Pee Wee.

"You know Aunt Sally. We get a Christmas card from her every year. It's a picture of a moose with tree lights strung on it."

"Oh," said Pee Wee. "Do you think she'll bring her moose?"

"It's not *her* moose, dummy, it's just a funny Christmas card," said Melissa.

"Nobody has a moose. What did you think—it was her pet or something?" said Amanda.

"A moose would make a nice pet," said Pee Wee.

"She's not bringing a moose," said Melissa.

The children returned to eavesdropping.

"Absolutely not, Doris!" Mr. Anderson said.

"It's only for one week, Robbie. Just one week. We don't want to forfeit our tickets!" pleaded Mrs. Anderson.

"Why do you think Daddy doesn't want to call Aunt Sally? Wait a second, he's picking up the phone," said Melissa.

"Maybe he's calling a kennel," said Pee Wee.

"THERE WILL BE NO KENNEL!" yelled Melissa so loudly that Mrs. Anderson, startled, made her way swiftly to the door and opened it.

"What are you doing here?" she asked sternly.

"Are you calling Aunt Sally?" asked Melissa.

"Can't your father and I ever have any privacy?"

"Aunt Sally doesn't really own a moose, does she?" asked Amanda.

"Didn't I put you to bed a long time ago?"

"Are you calling a kennel?" asked Pee Wee.

"Do you know how late it is?"

They stood staring at one another with a pile of unanswered questions between them until Mr. Anderson got off the phone and came to the door. He was pale.

"Guess who's coming Monday night?" he asked. "Aunt Sally from Canada."

Aunt Sally arrived late in the evening the night before Mr. and Mrs. Anderson left for Paris. Mr. Anderson went to pick her up at the airport. Mrs. Anderson made sure the house was clean, there were lots of groceries, and the children looked neat and tidy. Every time she passed Pee Wee, Mrs. Anderson brushed his long hair out of his eyes. It seemed pretty pointless to Pee Wee, as his hair always fell forward again, but it made his mother feel better.

"There she is! There she is!" called Mrs. Anderson when a pair of headlights came up the driveway. "Now look nice."

Amanda arranged her features in a nice expression. Melissa tucked her T-shirt in her jeans. Pee Wee wiped the hair out of his eyes himself.

Mrs. Anderson opened the door. "Why, Sally!" she said, and stood beaming at Aunt Sally as if she wasn't sure whether they were on kissing terms or not.

"Well, hello to you all! Bonjour, bonjour, as we of the bilingual country say," said Aunt Sally, grabbing Mrs. Anderson around the waist and pecking her heartily in the vicinity of her nose.

At first the children thought Aunt Sally was a giant. Then Melissa looked down and realized that Aunt Sally was wearing very high heels. The shoes were thick and chunky and had laces that wound around Aunt Sally's legs almost up to her knees. That was the bottom half of her. The top half was mostly very yellow hair that was piled way way up on top of her head like a tower. In between the top and the bottom was the gist of Aunt Sally. The gist was impressive enough. She had large, solid bones and more cheek space than most people. Her lips were thick and full. Her nose was a formidable entity and her eyes had more sparkles than normal sparkly eyes. There just seemed to be more altogether of Aunt Sally.

"These are the kids," said Mr. Anderson. The children thought he seemed kind of wary.

"They certainly are," said Aunt Sally. "Melissa, Amanda, and Frank, right?"

"We call him Pee Wee," said Melissa.

"Well, it's none of my business but I wouldn't let anyone call me that if my real name were Frank," said Aunt Sally, looking down at Pee Wee.

"Why not?" asked Pee Wee, who was pleased as punch to be the first one spoken to.

"Because then I couldn't say to someone, 'Let me be Frank!' It's a terrific play on words. Of course, it only works if everyone knows your name is Frank. 'Let me be Pee Wee!' isn't even remotely funny. Not even remotely. Besides which, it makes you sound short and you're not short, dear. You're a regular giant. Why, if a boy your age was that tall in Canada, they would make him skip grade school and go right into the Royal Canadian Mounted Police."

"Did you bring your moose with you?" asked Pee Wee.

"No, I did not," said Aunt Sally. "Where would I keep him—

in the bathtub? Not to mention trying to sneak him through customs."

"What's customs?" asked Amanda.

"It's a place where they open your suitcase and look at all your underwear," said Aunt Sally.

"Would you like to see your room?" said Mrs. Anderson, briskly leading Aunt Sally away.

"I don't believe she has a moose," said Melissa. "Does she, Daddy?"

"Oh, she was kidding," said their father. "I think. Now, how about some cookies and milk and then bed? Tomorrow's a school day and your mother and I want to have some quiet time with Aunt Sally to go over everything before we leave."

"Aw . . ." said Melissa.

"Daaaad . . ." said Amanda.

"I want to hear about her moose," said Pee Wee.

"A quick snack and bed," said Mr. Anderson, and that was that.

CLAM BITE!

Mr. and Mrs. Anderson left the next morning at the crack of dawn. The children shuffled around sadly during breakfast.

"Don't worry, they'll be fine," said Aunt Sally. "How'd you like to root through all my things when you get home from school. I won't even unpack."

The children nodded glumly but went off to school, feeling, as Amanda put it, a great missing lump in her stomach. When school got out, they still had great missing lumps but they were able to look forward to getting home and ransacking Aunt Sally's personal belongings.

True to her word, Aunt Sally hadn't unpacked. The children went into her bedroom and bounced on the bed next to the unopened suitcases. They waited shyly for Aunt Sally to suggest they open them.

"Well," said Melissa finally, talking to the ceiling but really directing her words at Aunt Sally, "what shall we do?"

"I don't know," said Aunt Sally. "There doesn't seem to be any real snooping protocol."

"What's a protocol?" asked Pee Wee, who thought it might be a large tool of some sort.

"It's sort of a formal agreement about things, such as: first we will examine all of Aunt Sally's socks and then we'll see if she brought any old love letters," said Aunt Sally. "Well, let's see now. What do we have here?" She opened the smaller suitcase, which was a hard-sided affair. "Ah yes, my makeup and jewelry case. I don't suppose you're interested in that."

"Yes we are," said Melissa.

"How do you get your hair like that?" asked Amanda.

"My beehive bubble, you mean? Very tricky. Both of you girls have long hair. You could do your hair like this."

"Show us on Pee Wee," said Melissa.

"Yes, demonstrate on Pee Wee," said Amanda.

Pee Wee looked alarmed.

"I'll do no such thing," said Aunt Sally. "Frank is far too devastatingly handsome to mess with. Now, you girls sit on the bed and I'll show you how to tease your hair. Here, Frank, I've got a bunch of different-colored eyeliner pencils and eye shadow that would make dandy crayons. You can draw pictures on this memo pad and offer insightful comments on my hairstyling."

"Oooo, can we have the eyeliners for a second?" said Melissa. Aunt Sally had taken out a whole handful in yellow, green, purple, and orange.

"I never saw so many colors of eyeliner," said Amanda.

"I have eyeliner and eye shadow to match all my clothes. Even my swimsuit," said Aunt Sally.

"You wear eyeliner with your swimsuit?" asked Melissa.

"Sure, you never know who you're going to meet at the beach," said Aunt Sally.

"Here, Pee Wee, let me see," said Melissa.

"Now, girls, let Frank have the eyeliner. We're doing *your* hair."

Aunt Sally teased and fluffed. "I'd better hurry," she said, "because your mother gave me a schedule and it says right here that at four-thirty Melissa has to practice her violin."

"I don't, really," said Melissa. "I mean, sometimes I can skip a day or two."

"Well, I know all kids hate to practice, and musical instruments have been known to be pretty dangerous."

"What do you mean, dangerous?" asked Pee Wee, looking up from the monster he had drawn with purple eyeliner and was now filling in with orange eye shadow.

"Surely your father has told you about the great disaster of 1967? On Vancouver Island, where we grew up? Surely he has told you about that?"

"No," said Amanda.

"Doesn't he tell you anything about growing up?" asked Aunt Sally.

"Well, some," said Amanda.

"Not much," said Melissa.

"Fancy that," said Aunt Sally, sweeping Amanda's hair into swirls, building a tower of hair higher and higher. "I suspect he doesn't want to scare you."

"Are instruments in Canada dangerous? Where is Canada? Is Canada on Vancouver Island?" asked Pee Wee.

"Hush," said Melissa. "If we told you where Canada was, it would be of no help to you whatsoever. Let Aunt Sally tell us about the dangerous instruments."

"Frank, dear, we'll get out a map later and I'll show you where Canada is. Canada is a big country and Vancouver Island is on its west coast. Right above Washington State."

"That'll be no help to him, he doesn't know where Washington State is," said Melissa.

"He doesn't know where anything is," said Amanda.

"I know where Ohio is," said Pee Wee.

"Of course you do, Frank. Now, where was I? It was the spring of 1967 and it all started with my brother, your Uncle John. John was a violinist, like you, Melissa. And like you he didn't enjoy practicing. But he did anyway, although when the weather got nice he sometimes forgot because he was too busy playing Here Come the Caribou!—that's a Canadian game."

"Will you teach us to play it?" asked Pee Wee.

"Stop interrupting," said Melissa.

"Yeah, shush up, Pee Wee," said Amanda.

"I'd be happy to, Frank," said Aunt Sally. "Anyhow, that spring he was supposed to take his grade-two exam with the Royal Academy of Music. The Royal Academy of Music was based in England, which to a lot of Canadians was still a link with respectability. If you studied an instrument, your parents could pay an enormous fee for you to take an exam with the Royal Academy. It was a big deal. You show up and do your stuff for some traveling hotshot. If you passed, you got a certificate and could go on to the next level the following year, and if you failed, you jumped off a cliff or something, I guess, because after your parents had paid those exam fees you had darn well better pass. Also, it was a reflection on your teacher, who was often housing the visiting examiner, so if you failed you humiliated not only yourself but pretty much everyone who had ever known you.

"John liked playing his pieces, but the scales almost drove him nuts. He had to remember all this tricky icky stuff about which fingers went where going up and going down. He studied and studied, but he always quit practicing before he got to the b-flat melodic minor. Now, myself, I think it was just the name that got to him. It sounded so devilishly difficult—b-flat melodic minor—it's a name that says, 'Don't even bother messing with me because I'm just too hard for words.' As the exam got closer, John grew more and more afraid of the b-flat melodic minor. Instead of concentrating on learning it, he began to work full-out on avoiding it. His teacher didn't understand why he couldn't learn it; he seemed to have learned everything else for the exam. He was a bright boy. But she need only say the name—b-flat melodic minor—for John to turn green. She was a nice lady, so she just patiently went over it again and again, lesson after lesson. This didn't help; John was so sure he couldn't learn it that his mind froze whenever she worked on it with him, so that as soon as he left her house he was unable to recall what they had done or how it went.

"As time passed, John went from being afraid of the b-flat melodic minor to being afraid of everything that was on the exam, until he stopped being able to practice at all. And, of course, all the time the exam got closer and closer. The exam fee was paid. There was no way he could wiggle out of it. No way at all. He lay in bed at night, tossing and turning and sweating and feeling utterly sick as his doom approached. Each advancing moment ticked b-flat melodic minor, b-flat melodic minor. Three days before the exam, he went down to the beach in a funk to sit on the rocks, wade in the shallows, and feel despair to the full. You know how when you're feeling real upset, sometimes you want a nice dramatic setting to feel despair to the full? The ocean's good for that. I don't know what you folks in Ohio do."

"I like to go to the dump," said Melissa.

"I like to sit in my closet," said Amanda.

"Nice and dark and dusty," said Aunt Sally. "And convenient!"

"I don't know what you're talking about," said Pee Wee.

"As usual," said Melissa.

"Well, anyhow, there he is on the beach absentmindedly poking rocks and catching crabs and stuff and he sticks his finger in a partly opened clam—something he had never done before and has never, believe you me, done since—and the clam bites him! I kid you not. John hollers and tries to slide his finger out, but the clam clamps down on the tip of his index finger and takes it right off."

"Oh, that's horrible!" said Amanda.

"You bet it's horrible," said Aunt Sally. "The poor kid thinks he's going to be sick. The tip is missing and his finger is bleeding for all it's worth. He runs up the path to our house, comes crashing through the door, crying, carrying on, and my father, your Grandpa Willie, sees his finger and says, 'My God, how did this happen, boy?' John cries, 'A clam bit me!' Well, your Grandpa Willie was the nicest man who ever lived. There wasn't a gentler, kinder, or better-liked man. And although usually a little vague and slow to act, he saw what some clam had done to his boy and he saw red. He picks up the rifle that we kept for cougars and bears, and rushes down, finds the clam, and shoots it."

"How did he know which clam it was?" asked Pee Wee.

"Why, it was the clam with the little piece of John's finger sticking out of its mouth. Meanwhile, your Grandma Evelyn takes John to Doctor Hanson, who patches up his finger and says that it will heal fine but he won't be able to use it for a few months. And that's when it hits him: he is out of the exam. He is saved. Uncle John sleeps his first good sleep in months. He and his teacher have to explain to the examiner that a clam has bitten him, and of course no one wants to believe him at first, but he has a doctor's note, and that's the end of that. Eventually John got over his fear of the b-flat melodic minor and went on to be quite a good violinist as well as learning that if you're afraid of something it's better to face it head-on than suffer the clam bites thereof."

"And no one ever stuck their finger in a clam again," said Melissa.

"*Everyone* stuck their fingers in clams after that. Do you think John was the only child in town afraid of his music exam? Violinists headed for the beach, pianists smeared cat food on their fingertips and headed for the cougar-filled woods, calling, 'Here, kitty kitty kitty.' One trumpet player was seen looking for a bear to kiss. Yes, you could always tell when it was Royal Academy exam time on Vancouver Island, because the woods and beaches were full of children trying to get their limbs bitten off."

"You're teasing," said Melissa.

"Well, anyhow, that's the way I recall it," said Aunt Sally. "That's how it was in the spring of '67. I could go on and on, but it's four-thirty and"—Aunt Sally paused and surveyed her masterpieces—"isn't your hair something?"

Melissa and Amanda looked at their towering hairdos.

"I wish I had some long dangling earrings like yours," Melissa said.

"Well, you can't wear them and play the violin. I remember Uncle John's teacher always made the girls take off all their jewelry before a recital."

"Then Uncle John really did play the violin?" asked Amanda.

"Oh, you bet he did. And he really did get bitten by a clam. That's Canada for you. Our motto is 'Ourus Clambitidio Rabido O Very Rabido'—loosely translated, 'Watch Out for the Clams.' Come, Frank, let's find an atlas and show you where your neighbor to the north is."

"I suppose you're going to have one of your nightmares, Pee Wee, thinking about those rabid clams," said Melissa.

"Yeah, and children trying to get cougars and bears to bite their hands off," said Amanda.

"I know Aunt Sally made that whole part up," said Pee Wee, putting down his monster drawing to get the atlas with Aunt Sally.

"Of course he knows that," said Aunt Sally. "Because he's much smarter than you girls give him credit for. I do believe he'll grow up to be President of the United States."

"I'd never stick my finger in any clam's mouth, that's for sure," scoffed Pee Wee.

"Never say you'd never do something. You have no idea the things you are capable of doing. Always, always keep that in mind," said Aunt Sally.

A sudden chill went inexplicably through the girls, the way a sudden breeze makes ripples on a lake, and then it was gone.

"Come, Frank," said Aunt Sally, and led him away to find the book.

GREENS!

While Melissa practiced her violin, Amanda tried on all of Aunt Sally's jewelry, Pee Wee used up the rest of Aunt Sally's eye shadow on monster pictures, and Aunt Sally made dinner. At six, when she called the children into the kitchen, they took one look, whiffed, and felt homesick for their mother again. There were string beans and a strange chicken mess on their plates. It was red and greasy and bore not the slightest resemblance to their mother's dinners, but they were too well-bred to let on. Amanda and Melissa smiled false, brave smiles and sat down.

Pee Wee said, "I'm not eating green beans."

"This looks good, what is it?" interrupted Melissa quickly.

"It's chicken paprikash," said Aunt Sally. "Yum-yum."

"I'm not eating any beans," said Pee Wee again.

"Oh, chicken paprikash!" said Amanda brightly. "Is that a Canadian dish?"

"No, if you want a Canadian dish, I'll make you sugar pie," said Aunt Sally.

"What's in sugar pie?" asked Melissa.

"Uh-uh. No beans," said Pee Wee.

"Maple sugar," said Aunt Sally.

"No beans at all," said Pee Wee.

"Quite right, never do anything for your health," said Aunt Sally. "Our old family doctor, Doc Hanson, always said that. Well, don't mind me." She stuck her fork in Pee Wee's beans and put them on her own plate.

"Never do anything for your health?" said Amanda. "What kind of doctor says that?"

"The kind who wonders: if life must be short, must it also be dreary? The vitamins in a bean are not worth the drudgery of the dreaded chew chew chew. Of course, it says on your mother's very thorough list that I must make you children eat your vegetables, but I do not see how I can possibly do that, do you?"

"No," said Amanda.

"Would you like mine as well?" asked Melissa.

"How *kind* of you to offer, Melissa. As there are only a limited number of beans in the house, should they not go to the bean lovers as opposed to the bean haters?"

"In that case, take mine," said Amanda, picking hers up and putting them on Aunt Sally's plate.

"Ah," said Aunt Sally, taking a bean delicately in her fingers and making gentle swoops and swirls in the air, then nibbling it, tiny bite after tiny bite, with voluptuous pleasure. "Now that we have the bean question resolved, we can all relax."

The children, having won so easily the bean war, ate their chicken paprikash in absentminded confusion.

"My mom always makes me eat all my beans," said Pee Wee.

"No doubt, no doubt," said Aunt Sally. "That is, no doubt, because she is such a good mother. As you can see, I would make a terrible mother. All my children would be gangrenous little snots. On the other hand, I have been permanently impressed by your Great-uncle Louis, who came for two weeks and stayed for six years. He used to make us children eat all our beans, too. For our health. Also bulrushes, which in Canada is a vegetable, served steamed and buttered. Also fiddleheads and seaweed and certain bushes in bush season. I used to get tired of the bushes myself. But your Uncle Edward absolutely loathed fiddleheads. Have you ever had them?"

"No," said Melissa.

"Well, that's a pity, really, because they look just like the head of a fiddle, that curling-around part? That's why they're called fiddleheads. They're one of your more attractive vegetables. You do get the feeling they're really *trying* to make up for the undeniable vitaminy taste. We had them quite a bit, fresh or frozen. Edward *despised* them. He despised them, but your Great-uncle Louis, who came for two weeks and stayed for six years, was on a health kick. He made us get up every morning at six to touch our toes. On a really vigorous day, we had to touch other people's toes. Everyone had to drink sixteen glasses of water a day and chew on sticks for fiber. We kept a large bowl of sticks in the living room, and after dinner we were expected to retire there to gnaw. Well, Edward didn't mind any of this, but he wouldn't eat his fiddleheads, which he said tasted like, well, never mind."

Aunt Sally picked up a bean and ran it under her nose like a good cigar, then she very delicately licked the tip of it.

"One night we were having fiddleheads for dinner and—Frank, you'll appreciate this—Edward says, 'I'm not eating these fiddleheads.' Well, Great-uncle Louis looks over and says, 'WHAT?!' "

Aunt Sally said this so loud that all three children jumped in their seats. They had finished their chicken paprikash and were watching Aunt Sally's devotion to her beans. She appeared to be cleaning her teeth with one. Melissa's fingers itched for a bean. A bean to play with. It was almost unbearable. She tried playing with her fork, but it was a poor substitute. Dare she ask Aunt Sally for one of her beans back? She dared not.

"Edward says, 'I will never eat another fiddlehead as long as I live.'

"Great-uncle Louis, who came for two weeks and stayed for

six years, stands up and shouts, 'What is the matter with this boy, Evelyn! Doesn't he want to be healthy? Doesn't he appreciate his Uncle Louis bringing sound nutrient ways to the family? Listen, Edward, you're sitting at that table until you eat every last fiddlehead, and someday you will thank me.' "

Aunt Sally stopped, because she was eating two beans at once, one out of each side of her mouth. She looked like a walrus consuming its own tusks. Pee Wee started to reach for a couple of beans but stopped. Even he knew you shouldn't grab food off your guest's plate. He shredded his napkin instead. Nobody had told him he could play walrus with his beans. That put a whole new complexion on the bean issue.

"Your Grandma Evelyn didn't want to contradict a grownup or a guest, even if it was her own brother, so she just sat there, looking uncomfortable. She and your Grandpa Willie ran a pretty happy-go-lucky household and this business of sitting at the table until you finished your vegetables wasn't their style. She kept trying to change the subject, hoping Great-uncle Louis, who came for two weeks and stayed for six years, would forget all about the fiddlehead matter. She tried suggesting that we leave the table and go into the living room to gnaw on sticks for a while, but Great-uncle Louis would have none of it. 'Evelyn,' he said, 'that boy must be taught healthy habits.' "

The sun had set and the kitchen was warm and cheerful in the glow of the overhead light. Normally, by now the children would have washed the dishes and would be sitting in front of the television. Instead, they sat cross-legged and every which way on their chairs, listening to Aunt Sally and watching her absorption with her beans. She held one like a pencil and scratched her nose with it.

"Edward said he would never eat the fiddleheads, so he guessed he'd be at that table forever. Great-uncle Louis said that he guessed they would all sit there forever, because no one was going to move until Edward had eaten his healthful fiddleheads. And there we sat."

Aunt Sally stopped to tilt her head back, raise her hand over her head, and drop beans into her open mouth like clothespins into a bottle. She didn't miss once. How we could use her at birthday parties, thought Amanda.

"Then I guess something in Edward broke, because he stood up on his chair and roared, 'I AM NEVER GOING TO EAT A SINGLE FIDDLEHEAD AND SO THERE!' At which point he made a daring leap over the table, knocking the mashed potatoes into Lyla's lap and sending John sprawling. Great-uncle Louis was after him like a shot, grabbing a handful of fiddleheads on his way, waving them wildly over his head and calling, 'Come back! Come back and eat these fiddleheads, you cur!' Grandma Evelyn kept saying, 'Oh, not a cur, surely, Louis?' in her mild tone. Grandpa Willie, who always looked a bit abstracted, murmured, 'Hmmm, wouldn't have thought fiddleheads could cause such a ruckus, myself. Fiddleheads, hmmm.'

"Edward raced up the stairs to the third floor, where he leapt out the bedroom window and slid down the drainpipe. Great-uncle Louis, who came for two weeks and stayed for six years, trailed him by a hair, overturning furniture and calling, 'Boy, don't get my dander up!' Both Great-uncle Louis and Edward scraped a good deal of their skin sliding down the drainpipe, and Great-uncle Louis landed directly on *top* of Edward. He looked down at Edward's squashed body, offered him the fiddleheads, and said, 'Boy, don't you know what's good for you?' Edward was naturally a lot younger and sprier than Great-uncle Louis, and he was able to roll out from under him while Great-uncle Louis, who had twisted an ankle, tried to shove the fiddleheads directly into Edward's mouth, hollering, 'They're full of vitamins, boy! They're full of vitamins!'

"Edward headed straight for our old rowboat, which was docked on the creek that ran through our property. Great-uncle Louis hobbled behind on his sprained ankle. Edward would have gotten away had not a family of raccoons taken up residence in the rowboat, so that when Edward jumped into it, they all shot up from under the seats. The raccoons caused a great chattering commotion, and the father raccoon bit Edward on the leg. Edward hopped around frantically, which gave Uncle Louis just enough time to make a daring leap into the rowboat, babbling, 'And the fiber, boy! Think of the fiber. Are you mad to avoid such fibrous vegetation, you little anti-herbivore?!'

"Edward, who was stunned from the raccoon bite, wasn't thinking clearly, because he grabbed the oars and began pulling for all he was worth, taking Great-uncle Louis *with* him. The suddenness of Edward's action caused the boat to lurch. Great-uncle Louis lost his balance and almost fell overboard, but instead got the side of the boat WHACK in his stomach, which made him lose his breath and retch six or seven times before recovering enough to yell, 'Gives your hair a shine, too! *Think* of what you'll save on pomade!' Of course, Edward didn't know what pomade was, because it was before his time."

"What is it?" asked Pee Wee.

"Hair grease," said Aunt Sally. "Turned out the boat had some holes in it and sank right then and there, with Great-uncle Louis trying desperately to hang on to his handful of fiddleheads. Edward, who had his hands free, swam to shore. Of course, they both had hypothermia by now, because it was winter and the creek was freezing cold. Edward struggled up and ran, a clear-and-clean getaway. Uncle Louis was drowning, because he wouldn't release his handful of fiddleheads, but he still managed to call to the fleeing Edward, 'Have you tried them with butter, boy? A little salt and pepper?'

"Edward turned around to give Great-uncle Louis a look, because most of his sentence had dissolved into 'blub blub blub' as he went under for the third time, and in glancing back he didn't see a tree root, fell over, and split his head open on a rock in the path. When Grandpa Willie and Grandma Evelyn finally caught up to them, hauled them both up, and got them to the doctor, poor Doc Hanson didn't know what to attend to first, the hypothermia, the sprained ankle, the raccoon bite, the missing skin, the near-drownedness, or the split-open head."

"I'm sorry," Melissa interrupted, "but are there any more beans in the pan?"

"No, I don't believe so," said Aunt Sally, who was using two beans as knitting needles, knit knit knit, nibble nibble nibble. " 'My God,' Doc Hanson says, 'how did this happen?'

"So then Grandma Evelyn tells him about the fiddleheads.

" 'Vitamins!' moaned what was left of Great-uncle Louis.

"That's when Doc Hanson says, 'Never do anything for your health.' "

Aunt Sally popped the last bean in her mouth, smiled, and burped.

"Excuse me," she said.

"I want beans," said Pee Wee.

"Beans, Frank? Surely not. You know what we'd have then— FRANK AND BEANS!" said Aunt Sally, pounding the table in mirth.

"Please, can you make some more beans and tell some more stories?" asked Melissa, bending over to address Aunt Sally, who was giggling, her forehead resting against the kitchen table.

"We need beans. We need many beans, now," said Amanda, who wanted to knit and nibble.

"You are the strangest children I ever saw," said Aunt Sally, lifting her head to look at them. "If you wanted beans, why did you give me yours? There aren't any more beans. Your mother left only that one bag. How about some ice cream instead?"

"Can't we go to the grocery store? We have time before bedtime," said Amanda.

"It's too far to walk at this hour, and anyhow it'll be closed by now, I would think," said Aunt Sally.

"We can at least check," said Pee Wee.

"Wait, maybe we can order out," said Melissa. "What about Chinese food, do they have beans?"

"Not green beans," said Amanda. "We could get pea pods, but I don't think it would be the same."

"Maybe there are some cans of beans in the cupboard," said Amanda, getting a chair, climbing on the counter, and searching the top shelves.

"Maybe there's some in the big freezer," said Melissa, running downstairs.

"Maybe there's some in the fridge, behind other things," said Pee Wee, opening the refrigerator and throwing things out over his shoulder in the hunt for hidden beans.

"Hey!" said Aunt Sally when a herring landed on her foot. But no one found any beans.

"It's awfully late," said Aunt Sally. "Your mother says right here that Frank has to be in bed by seven-thirty."

"No beans," said Melissa.

"I can't stand it. I don't know if I can sleep tonight," said Amanda, her fingers still itching for the feel of a long thin bean.

"Can you please, please shop for more beans tomorrow?" asked Melissa, as she and Amanda went upstairs and Pee Wee went to bed.

"Gosh, I feel like such a beast, eating all those beans myself," said Aunt Sally. "And on your mother's very thorough timetable it suggests we have broccoli tomorrow."

"You can't be a walrus with broccoli," said Pee Wee.

"You can't knit with broccoli," said Amanda.

"You can't scratch your nose with it, either," said Melissa.

"I'm not eating any broccoli," said Pee Wee.

"More," said Aunt Sally, "for me."

DANGER ON VANCOUVER ISLAND!

As Aunt Sally tucked Pee Wee in bed, Melissa and Amanda found themselves hanging around his bedroom door, not wanting to miss any stories.

"How come Daddy never told us about the clam bite or Great-uncle Louis who came for two weeks and stayed for six years?" asked Pee Wee.

"I don't know for sure," said Aunt Sally, "but I suspect it's because of the solemn vow."

"What's a vow?" asked Pee Wee.

"It's a promise, Pee Wee," said Melissa. "Now shhh."

"What promise?" asked Pee Wee.

"Haven't you ever noticed that Americans know nothing about Canada? It's just a big mystery to you folks down here," said Aunt Sally.

"I *have* noticed that," said Melissa.

"Why is that?" asked Amanda.

"Because we choose to keep it that way," said Aunt Sally. "We all take a solemn vow every morning of our lives not to ever tell any Americans what goes on up there."

"What does?" asked Melissa.

"Parties!" said Aunt Sally.

"No!" said Melissa.

"I don't believe it!" said Amanda.

"As far as I can recall. Parties, noon and night."

"What kind of parties?" asked Pee Wee.

"The kind with cupcakes," said Aunt Sally.

"Oh, that kind," said Pee Wee. "How come they don't want us to know about their parties?"

"For a very good reason. Canada is a big country in terms of land, but it's not as big as the United States in terms of people or power, and Canadians always feel Americans are real people leading real lives and Canadians are but shadows or ghosts of the real people down south. It worries them. That's why, when you go to shopping malls close to the border, you see Canadians walking around looking absolutely terrified. They turn their heads from side to side, watching to see how Americans act. They restrain their impulse to leap into shopping carts and race each other up and down the halls. They contain their urge to jump into the center of dress racks. Because they are afraid Americans will think they are gauche."

"I never even think about Canadians," said Pee Wee.

"Yes, and that's *just what drives us wild*," said Aunt Sally.

"I'm hungry," said Melissa.

"Me, too," said Amanda.

"Me three," said Pee Wee.

"Oh, you disgusting little worm," said Melissa. "You know you're not hungry, you're just trying to get out of going to bed."

"Pardon me," said Aunt Sally, "but can you give me one good reason why you and Amanda can be hungry but Frank can't?"

"He's always pulling stunts like this," said Melissa. "Trying to stay up all night."

"Trying to monopolize Mom," said Amanda.

"I do not," said Pee Wee.

"You don't even know what monopolize means," said Melissa.

"I'M HUNGRY!" said Pee Wee.

"I'm afraid I have no more beans," said Aunt Sally. "But I'll make some cocoa. If everyone gets into bed, I will bring it to you."

"It's awfully early for me to go to bed," said Melissa.

"I'll tell you girls more about Canada. What fun—Aunt Sally makes geography come alive!" said Aunt Sally. "And tomorrow, Pee Wee, I'll tell *you* about Canada."

Aunt Sally went to the kitchen and made a big pan of cocoa, deposited some with Pee Wee, and then went into the room

Melissa and Amanda shared. She pulled up a chair between the twin beds and they all sipped cocoa and listened to the rain beginning to fall.

"Rain falling reminds me of Vancouver Island," said Aunt Sally. "Since your daddy has told you nothing about it, I don't suppose you know it rains there all year round except for summer, when the sun comes out and dries everything to a crisp."

"You mean, it doesn't snow in winter?" asked Amanda. "I thought Canada was covered in snow."

"Well, most of it is. *Mon pays ce n'est pas mon pays, c'est l'hiver.* Do you know what that means?"

The girls shook their heads.

"It means: My country is not my country, it is winter. They say that accounts a lot for who Canadians are, these long, dark winters. On the island we have long, dark, rainy winters, but the Japanese current—you probably don't know about that, either?"

The girls shook their heads.

"It's water that flows over from Japan, warming the island, so that it's rainy and foggy all winter, instead of snowy."

"That must be kind of depressing," said Amanda, thinking no sledding, no skating, no snowmen.

"No, it's not," said Aunt Sally. "You know what it's like? It's like living underwater. Did you ever go swimming in a lake or the ocean in the summer and the water is such a perfect temperature and it feels so good all around you, dripping from your bangs, swirling around your legs, wetting your lips, that you imagine yourself building a little house like a mermaid and living in the water forever, never getting out? And when you do finally get dragged back to land by your mother at the end of the day because she wants to go home and make supper, it is unbearable to leave the life and movement of the waves. That's how I feel in the rainy season. I am back to my childhood and I am swimming, swimming, dripping, submerged in water. Oh, how wearying it is when June comes and the sun shines long dusty day after day. In October, when the first foghorns begin to bellow the beginning of the rain, my long summer-sick soul awakes."

Amanda and Melissa looked at each other from their beds.

"My," said Melissa.

"You do have a way with words," said Amanda.

"Anyhow, when your daddy and I were growing up, we lived right in the middle of the woods. Have you seen the paintings by Emily Carr?"

The girls shook their heads again.

"She painted the woods around us. Huge, dark trees, great hollow echoes of quiet. Forests of Douglas fir going down to the ocean, where waves crash against boulders. Look one way and you see the tall Olympic Mountains, look another way and you see the jagged ghostly lavender outline of the Cascades."

"It sounds idyllic," said Melissa, who knew a lot of fancy words.

"It pretty much was," said Aunt Sally. "It pretty much still is."

"How come Daddy never tells us about it?" asked Amanda. "I mean, I know you were teasing about that solemn-vow business."

Aunt Sally finished her cocoa and looked slowly around the room.

"Well," she said, as though she were trying to decide whether to tell them something or not. Or maybe just trying to decide how to word it. For the first time Aunt Sally looked serious.

"I don't want to mention it around Frank. As you say, he has nightmares. But I suspect it's because of the trolls."

The girls sipped their cocoa and waited for Aunt Sally to go on. Amanda hoped she would tell them a long, outrageous story about trolls. Melissa wanted to see Aunt Sally's more-than-normally sparkly eyes do their thing, but they didn't. Instead, Aunt Sally looked out the window, where the rain was washing the big yellowing leaves off the oak tree.

"I don't want to give you girls nightmares, either," said Aunt Sally.

"Pff, I never get nightmares," said Melissa.

"Me, either. Hardly ever," said Amanda.

"I love living on Vancouver Island, but growing up there was especially wonderful," began Aunt Sally dreamily. "We had a big old clapboard house with a wraparound porch that was surrounded by trees, except for the side where our neighbors the Hoffners, who never spoke to us, lived. We had paths on our property that led down to the sea, and I'd get up every morning to run down to see the ocean. It got so I felt the tides wouldn't change without me. The ocean's different every morning. Sometimes it's pulled back, with hard flat sand to walk on and seagulls looking for mussels and clams to open by dropping them on rocks. Other times it's pulled up to shore like a bed that's just been made. Sometimes the sun sparkles on the water in a new-world way, and other times fog rolls in like a cozy fleece blanket over the beach.

"And I loved the woods, too. They were full of cougars and bears, of course. I never saw a cougar, though most people I knew had seen one. I saw a black bear once; it was running across the road and it ran so fast that I realized if I ever had an altercation—there's a word for you, Melissa—with a bear, the bear was going to win. Even now, the tourist bureau in town gives hikers bear pamphlets they can refer to as they run for their lives. What to do when you meet up with a bear in the woods—you can't outrun it, they warn you, bears can go thirty-five miles an hour or even faster. Don't try to escape by climbing a tree, because bears climb trees routinely. What should you—trying to be a responsible hiker and preserve your life—do? Don't bother playing dead, bears would just as soon pick at your lifeless body. You might try acting very big, waving your arms around over your head and making ferocious noises. It probably won't work, but you can't say you haven't given the venture your all. Their best advice is, try not to meet up with any bears in the woods. Have a nice hike. I never read one of those pamphlets without saying to myself, just what knothead printed this worthless thing anyway?"

"Did you ever know anyone who was eaten by a bear?" asked Amanda.

"No, I did not," said Aunt Sally. "And I always think the lack of sensational bear attacks comes as a constant disappointment to the person who distributes these pamphlets. One gets the feeling he simply lives for the day they find an entire disemboweled family."

"What's disemboweled?" asked Amanda.

"Gutted," said Melissa.

"Oh, gross," said Amanda.

"No sense mincing our words," said Aunt Sally. "Anyhow, we lived with these natural dangers. In Sooke, which wasn't far from us, they even had wolves. Still do. Imagine that, in this day and age. I knew about all these dangers, but if you love the woods you don't give them more than a thought now and then. Any more than you dwell on rogue waves crashing on you and carrying you out to sea, which happened to people I know. It was a nice family, Mom, Dad, three kids, Grandma, aunts, cousins—they took Grandpa to the beach for a picnic to celebrate his seventy-fifth birthday. They were packed up and heading back to the path up the hill when they happened to turn around just in time to see Grandpa being carried off in the undertow of a giant rogue wave. It had come up behind them suddenly, and only Grandpa, who had lagged slightly behind, was in its range. It swept him away as silently as if he had never existed. In truth, he didn't from then on. They never even found the body. Happy birthday to Grandpa."

"That's horrible," said Melissa.

"That makes me never want to go to the beach," said Amanda. "I'm going to have nightmares about rogue waves."

"Oh, for heaven's sakes," said Melissa. "Do you think some giant wave is going to wash over eight states to get to Ohio or something?"

"That would be some wave," agreed Aunt Sally. "I think tomorrow I'm going to build Frank a tree house."

"He always gets everything," said Amanda.

"We're too old for a tree house," said Melissa.

"In Canada, the prime minister lives in a tree house," said Aunt Sally. "It represents his commitment to the squirrels. You gotta love a country that is committed to its squirrels."

"I'm chilly," said Amanda. "That's so horrible about their grandfather. It's so terrible to think of something coming out of the clear blue sky and making you disappear."

"I know what you mean," said Aunt Sally, "but it's not the natural disasters you have to fear. It's the ones that are inside of you, waiting to happen, like what your Uncle John and Uncle Edward and I did to your father. But it's late. Look, it's after nine and on this very thorough list that your mother left me it says that you have to have lights out at nine. If I go on anymore, it will be ten before I finish *that* story."

Aunt Sally got up and collected the cocoa cups. She looked way out the bedroom window beyond the rain drenching the backyard and sighed. Then she switched off the bedside lamp, enclosing them in autumnal darkness.

THE NEW MRS. GUNDERSON!

The next day when the children got home from school they heard the sound of hammering and found Aunt Sally straddling a branch of the old oak tree in the backyard.

"I didn't have time to get beans today, but I've almost finished Frank's tree house," she said through a mouthful of nails.

"Oh, wow!" yelled Pee Wee, and climbed up the tree to inspect.

"Well, come on in, honey," said Aunt Sally. "Now all you need is a big obnoxious sign that says something like 'Frank's Tree House, Keep Out' or 'No Girls Allowed.' "

"Hey," said Amanda. "Don't give him ideas."

"Yeah," said Melissa. "He has enough ideas on his own. We try to keep him humble." She and Amanda giggled.

Aunt Sally and Pee Wee ignored them. "I've just got to put

the finishing touches on this and make sure all the side railings are secure."

"I don't need those," scoffed Pee Wee.

"Don't want you to meet the fate of Mrs. Gunderson," said Aunt Sally.

"Who was she?" asked Amanda from below.

"She was the dog who lived next door. Now, surely your father told you about the new Mrs. Gunderson?"

"No," said Melissa.

"Well, next door to us in the woods lived the Hoffners, a family of German immigrants that none of us liked. They were very stiff-necked, and always glared at us suspiciously when they saw us, which, considering that we were more or less isolated in the woods with them, was ultra-unfriendly. However, since our house was always overstuffed with people and activity and we didn't want for company, we pretty well ignored them."

"There was Aunt Lyla," said Amanda.

"And Uncle John and Uncle Edward," said Pee Wee.

"And you and Daddy," said Melissa. "And Grandma Evelyn and Grandpa Willie."

"And let us not forget Great-uncle Louis, who came for two weeks and stayed for six years. And assorted houseguests, and for a long time Aunt Hattie, who flitted through on weekends. Anyhow, as if that weren't enough, we begged and begged and begged for a dog, until one day Grandpa Willie got us one. A wonderful collie we named Tibby. The people next door had a dog, too. They had a beagle named Mrs. Gunderson that we all hated. She would come leaping out of the house and run down the porch steps barking six to the dozen every morning and every time anyone left our house. She was just a real dumb yappy little thing. She yapped at our puppy every morning and scared the poor thing to death. We expected Frau Hoffner next door to feed Tibby to her beagle at the first opportunity. We tried our best to keep her away from Mrs. Gunderson.

"But then one day as we were walking Tibby on a leash past their house, Frau Hoffner came out. 'Hello!' she called in her heavy German accent. *'Wie geht's?* And that's a fine beautiful little puppy you have.' She came waddling out to us, oozing maternal noises, and was all over our collie, petting her, talking baby talk to her, asking us where we had gotten her. I think it was the first time any of us had ever seen her smile. Well, we didn't know what to make of it. Every time Frau Hoffner saw us with the puppy, she would smile and wave and want to trade dog talk. Lyla, the sainted, said that it was only a matter of finding people's soft spots. Lyla never quite took the grim attitude toward the Hoffners that the rest of us did. She went around believing that everyone was misunderstood in this workaday world and it was only a matter of finding out *how* they were misunderstood—like finding the right key for a lock—and peace would come to our land. She figured that we had unlocked Frau Hoffner—she was a dog lover. Apparently, by buying a dog, we had revealed ourselves as slightly better than the scumbags Frau Hoffner had previously believed us to be. Edward and I thought that actually she still *did* think we were scumbags but was using us to get to Tibby. Even so, it was much more comfortable to have her waving to us from her porch and calling shrilly *'Wie geht's?'* than it was to have her casting disapproving looks in our general direction. Her husband and four hulking sons still didn't speak to us. They never seemed to speak to her, either. She had her large garden that she was always working on, with Mrs. Gunderson yapping at her heels, and that was pretty much her lot. I took to calling *'Wie geht's?'* now and again just to give her a little human contact.

"While this was all going on at the human level of discourse, at the *dog* level things remained unchanged; as soon as our puppy was let outside in the morning, Mrs. Gunderson came down the Hoffners' porch steps like thunder in a baking tin. One morning I heard the beginning of thunder, a yap, and then the most hideous keening and wails from Mrs. Gunderson. It sounded as if she were being tortured. It sounded as if she were being *eaten.* I thought of cougars and dashed out to make sure Tibby wasn't on the dessert menu. Most of the family was already on the porch and we all stared down at Frau Hoffner, who was kneeling over the prostrate body of Mrs. Gunderson.

" 'Can we help you, Frau Hoffner?' called Grandpa Willie. 'What has happened to Mrs. Gunderson?'

" 'She fell off our porch!' cried Frau Hoffner. 'We must take her to the animal hospital. Oh, my God, my God in heaven! Heinrich! Heinrich!' And she began to cry in a terrible grownup way.

"We all shuffled about self-consciously. Finally Heinrich appeared with a blanket; they scooped up Mrs. Gunderson and put her in their car.

"That's all we heard about it until evening. Edward and I made several grim jokes about Mrs. Gunderson's crutches. Mrs. Gunderson's wheelchair. We felt that tripping while racing down the porch steps was a kind of poetic justice and we hoped that when Mrs. Gunderson got back from the animal hospital she would be housebound for a few days to reflect upon her ways.

"That night at dinner, Grandpa Willie sat down and said, 'I saw Frau Hoffner this afternoon and she introduced me to the new Mrs. Gunderson.'

"There was a silence at the table.

" 'Mrs. Gunderson broke her back when she fell and had to be put down. Frau Hoffner has bought a new puppy. A collie this time. Evelyn, these are wonderful potatoes.'

"Edward and I looked at each other across the table. We felt like a couple of skunks. We never once, while making jokes, considered the possibility that Mrs. Gunderson might have been killed.

" 'She broke her back! How devastating,' said Grandma Evelyn. 'Frau Hoffner must be beside herself. That dog seemed to mean everything in the world to her.'

" 'I'd say *our* dog seems to mean everything in the world to her,' said Robbie.

" 'Whatever do you mean, Robbie?' asked Grandma Evelyn.

" 'Haven't you noticed how much she likes Tibby?' asked John.

" 'Well, yes, she did say that if she had it to do all over again she would get a collie,' said Grandma Evelyn.

" 'And now she has,' said Robbie. 'She has had it to do all over again and she's gotten her collie. I guess she's happy now.'

" 'Oh, don't say such things, Robbie,' said Lyla. 'I'm sure she's just sick with grief.'

" 'Nonsense, the woman's happy as a clam! Saw her outside today. Singing!' said Great-uncle Louis.

" 'If Tibby died I would cry my eyes out for years,' I said. 'I couldn't even look at another dog for weeks and weeks.'

" 'Well, we all grieve in our own fashion, Sally,' said Grandma Evelyn. 'Perhaps Frau Hoffner felt that the house would be unbearable without a dog and she got a puppy right away to take her mind off things.'

" 'If you ask me, she never liked the old Mrs. Gunderson much, anyway,' said Edward.

" 'Oh, I think she liked her, all right,' said John. 'I think she just liked our dog *better*. And then there's the matter of the rails.'

" 'What do you mean?' asked Grandma Evelyn.

" 'If you ask me, you ought to ride that whole family out of town on rails. Now, there's something I'd pay admission to see!' said Great-uncle Louis, wiping his dinner elaborately out of his mustache with his napkin.

" 'Louis, please,' said Grandma Evelyn.

" 'What's for dessert?' asked Great-uncle Louis.

" 'Rice pudding,' said Grandma Evelyn.

" 'Bah! I'm going camping on the island,' said Great-uncle Louis, and he went clomping off.

" 'What rails?' said Grandma Evelyn.

" 'That's how she did it, you know,' said John. 'The dog didn't trip going down those stairs. The dog knew those stairs like the back of her paw. No, I saw Frau Hoffner take all the side rails off last night.'

" 'How dreadful,' said Grandma Evelyn. 'I suppose they hadn't replaced them with new rails yet and the poor dog fell off the side. How doubly terrible for Frau Hoffner, she must feel responsible.'

" 'But she didn't replace them with *new* rails,' said John. 'Because I hid on our porch this afternoon when I heard hammering and I *watched*. She put *the same rails back on*.'

"Grandma Evelyn stared at him blankly for a minute while we all digested this. 'What are you saying, John?' she finally asked in her quiet voice.

" 'It wasn't an accident,' John hissed. 'It was *murder!*' "

" 'She murdered her dog?" said Melissa in disbelief.

"It was the side rails that reminded me," said Aunt Sally. "You see how important they are, Frank? So don't yank them off, dear. Now I'd better go see about dinner."

"She murdered her dog?" repeated Amanda later after they had all finished eating and the girls supervised Pee Wee as he cleaned the kitchen.

"You missed a spot," snapped Melissa. "And don't drop the dish towel on the floor and then use it again on the dishes, you little pig."

"Did you girls clean the kitchen when you were only six?" asked Aunt Sally.

"Yes," said Melissa.

"Absolutely," said Amanda.

"And vacuumed."

"And dusted."

"And made our beds."

"And raked the leaves."

"And did a lot of heavy lifting."

"I see," said Aunt Sally. "Well, come, Frank, I say it's bedtime. I'll finish up your work later after everyone is in bed."

She led Pee Wee away to give him a bedtime geography lesson about Canada, with the girls making faces behind his back.

When Amanda and Melissa got into bed, Aunt Sally came in and sat in the rocker between their beds.

"Tell us the story you started last night," said Melissa.

"Yes, tell us about growing up on Vancouver Island," said Amanda.

"Tell us more stories about cougars and bears and giant waves," said Melissa.

"Oh, cougars and bears and giant waves!" scoffed Aunt Sally. "That was nothing. Tonight I'm going to tell you about the trolls."

WHAT GREAT-UNCLE LOUIS SAW!

"Well," said Aunt Sally when she was settled in the rocking chair between the twin beds. "After your Uncle John announced his suspicions about the rails, we spent the next few nights having lively dinnertime conversations about the old and the new Mrs. Gunderson and whether the Hoffners had murdered their dog. We were deprived of the opinion of Great-uncle Louis, who came for two weeks and stayed for six years, because after stomping out of dinner he went back to Cooter's Island, which was just off our beach, to camp out and fish for a week. He did this from time to time and claimed it was for his physical health, but we thought it was most likely for his mental health, as sometimes I think the lot of us drove him clean mad. He had a secret store of Mackintosh's toffee in his bedroom and always took it with him to the island."

"What's Mackintosh's toffee?" asked Melissa.

"Oh, just the world's best toffee. It comes in a flat bar about the width of your hand. You suck on it and let it engage in wrestling matches with your teeth and generally end up with toffee and drool all over yourself."

"Well, that doesn't sound very healthy," said Amanda.

"I suspect he knew that, which is why he hid it in his room. Of course, we kids always snooped about his room whenever his back was turned. We were probably trying to repay him for making our house into an institute of health, because we never did anything like that to Aunt Hattie or any other houseguest that I can remember. Anyhow, when he came back from the island finally and we were all eating the herring he had caught and discussing the murder of Mrs. Gunderson yet again, he piped up, 'I'll go you one further. That woman didn't take her dog to the vet to be put down. She gave it to the trolls.'

" 'To the what?' we all cried in amazement.

" 'To the trolls,' said Great-uncle Louis. 'Oh, I've seen them many a time on my camping trips. They don't usually come out in the daytime. And if they do, they are hard to see because they lean against the shale ledges and blend in, for they have faces of stone. No mouths, leathery skin black as night, and eyes like emeralds. When they close their lids, they can be the craggy dark cliffs or the charred hollows of trees, but when they open them, you catch their jewel-like eyes shining in the darkness of their visages.' "

"What's a visage?" asked Amanda.

"Face," said Melissa. "Now shhh."

" ' "Give us your garbage," say the trolls who scavenge the beach, "but you will never get it back," ' said Great-uncle Louis."

"How could they say anything if they didn't have mouths?" asked Amanda.

"That's exactly what your Uncle Edward asked your Great-uncle Louis, and you know what he said?"

"What?" asked Amanda breathlessly.

"What?" asked Melissa with large eyes.

"He said, 'Eat your bulrushes and shut up.' He wasn't always the most patient or polite of men. Then Grandma Evelyn piped up, 'Now, don't scare the children, Louis. Don't go telling them nonsense stories of trolls.'

" 'NONSENSE?' cried Great-uncle Louis, 'NONSENSE? Is that what you call it, that which I tell you plainly I saw with my own eyes? Well, your Frau Hoffner doesn't think it nonsense. The morning Mrs. Gunderson broke her back, I went down to the island to fish. There I was, casting off a rock, when I saw Frau Hoffner bring that poor animal down to the beach. The trolls came and got Mrs. Gunderson, hunching their crooked-back way along the shore, carrying her away in their knotted, gnarled hands.'

" 'Why didn't you tell us this the other night?' asked Edward.

" 'I said I saw the woman singing, didn't I?' said Great-uncle Louis.

" 'You didn't say why or where,' said John. 'You didn't mention any trolls, either.'

" 'I was biding my time,' said Great-uncle Louis, leaning back in his chair and looking down his nose at us.

" 'Well, if she was going to give her dog to the trolls, why'd she bother to break its back?' asked Edward.

" 'Because her mind is diseased!' said Great-uncle Louis. 'From lack of greens!'

"Edward made a snorting sound of disbelief and Great-uncle Louis bellowed, 'Are those bulrushes I see on your plate, sir?!'

" 'Let's all settle down some,' said Grandpa Willie.

" 'Well, I think Frau Hoffner was just devastated when Mrs. Gunderson died,' said Lyla.

" 'As devastation goes, it was pretty darn short,' said John.

" 'Yeah, like less than twenty-four hours,' I said.

" 'And I certainly don't believe in silly mythical creatures like trolls,' Lyla went on. She was the oldest of us and long past fairy stories.

" 'There's nothing silly about them, girl. They answer to the blackest evil in our hearts,' said Great-uncle Louis.

" 'Oh, Louis, stop,' said Grandma Evelyn again.

" 'The children should know about evil, Evelyn,' said Great-uncle Louis. 'To guard against it. We must be ever vigilant. AND. EAT. OUR. GREENS!'

"Then we all went into the living room to gnaw on sticks. We were gnawing away when Great-uncle Louis said, 'I've seen many, with minds diseased from lack of greens, hauling their loved ones down to meet the trolls.'

" 'I don't think Reverend McKinley, or any of the other pastors in town, would approve of this talk, Louis,' said Grandma Evelyn. 'I'm sure there's enough frightening evil in the world without making up trolls, for mercy's sake.'

" 'Reverend McKinley, Reverend McKinley! I say it's a good thing you aren't a parishioner at *his* church. *There's* a man who's left a few things for the trolls,' said Great-uncle Louis.

" 'Louis, please,' said Grandma Evelyn.

" 'Well, if you don't want to face facts, Evelyn, I'll not be responsible,' said Great-uncle Louis, and he broke into two sticks at once with great cracking noises.

"Grandma Evelyn didn't mind us gnawing sticks, but she always winced when Great-uncle Louis crunched two at once and spit pieces of bark into the fire. She murmured something about mending to tend to and left the living room.

" 'What did he leave to the trolls?' asked Robbie.

" 'His wives, for starters. All four of them,' said Great-uncle Louis. 'Barnyard animals, compost, rotten leather harnesses. Once he got started, there was no stopping him.'

" 'Why did he leave compost?' asked John. 'No one throws out compost.'

" 'Because the trolls wanted it. Quite a little relationship he had developed with those trolls after wife number four. They took *her* away . . . screaming,' said Great-uncle Louis.

" 'Oh, honestly,' said Lyla, and this time she left the room.

" 'Why would he give her away?' asked Robbie. 'Why would he give any of them away?'

" 'Well, I guess that's just his little secret, isn't it? Pass me another stick. Darned good sticks tonight.'

" 'I don't believe it,' snorted Edward.

" 'And that's just for starters,' continued Great-uncle Louis. 'There was the Billings family. Now, that was a sorry thing to witness. I was on the island, hoping for a peaceful evening, when down comes little Amanda Billings, dragging her teddy bear. She leaves it for the trolls and goes back up the hill. I shook my head sorrowfully. An innocent mistake of youth? No! There's a child, I said to myself, who has pushed away her spinach one too many nights. It ate away at her brain. It corroded her very being. It *annoyed* her parents.'

" 'How do you know?' asked Edward. 'Maybe they didn't like spinach either. A lot of people don't like spinach.'

" 'Silence! The next night, who should come down the hill but Amanda Billings's babysitter, dragging Amanda and leaving her on shore. The plot thickens, I said to myself. An hour later Mr. and Mrs. Billings came down, dragging Amanda's babysitter. The babysitter cried, "I didn't want to do it, but she kept asking and asking for juice! How many times can I be expected to pour juice?! Sometimes I'd pour it and she wouldn't even drink it!" But Mr. and Mrs. Billings didn't give a fig for excuses. Then the babysitter's parents brought Mr. and

Mrs. Billings down. Then Grandma and Grandpa Billings brought the babysitter's parents down. Revenge, you see, revenge gone mad. Then . . .'

" 'This is just getting silly,' interrupted Edward. 'You can't drag struggling adults down to the beach that easily.'

" 'Spoken like a bulrush avoider. If you'd seen what I'd seen! Old women leaving their ancient mothers on shore! In-laws piled up like kindling! It was a dark season the springtime of the Billings Revenge. Like a disease. Soon the whole town might have been destroyed, left to the scavengers, but something stopped it.'

" 'What?' asked Edward skeptically.

" 'The arrival of the fresh asparagus! Ten cents a pound. Who could resist? Soon everyone was eating it. It put a stop to the madness.'

" 'Are you trying to say a whole town was saved from evil by a new crop of asparagus?' asked John, choking with barely suppressed giggles.

" 'Yes, I've seen it all,' said Great-uncle Louis, who either didn't hear John or chose to ignore him. 'I've seen it all from Cooter's Island. *And I saw that woman bring her dog down and give it to the trolls and go up the hill again, singing.*'

"We sat silently for a moment, listening to the crackle of the fire. Finally Robbie said, 'I believe you, Great-uncle Louis. I believe Frau Hoffner gave Mrs. Gunderson to the trolls.'

" 'Aye, Robbie, you always were the pick of the litter,' said

Great-uncle Louis, which was bad enough, but next thing we knew, he had given your daddy a Mackintosh's toffee bar. Well, your daddy was the spoiled baby in the family. John and Edward and I glanced at each other, the same dark thoughts prowling our minds . . . Look at the time. I better turn out your light."

"What dark thoughts?" asked Melissa.

"Why don't you ever *finish* a story?" asked Amanda.

"Oh, great, now *I'm* going to have nightmares. Trolls. It's that part about them having no mouths," said Melissa.

"Are all the doors locked?" asked Amanda.

"There are no locks to keep out the trolls," said Aunt Sally. "But don't worry, the trolls don't come to you. It's your own darkness that leads you to the trolls."

She stood up, turned out the light, and the girls heard her earrings jangling all the way downstairs.

THE EARTHQUAKE SAFETY POSTER
CONTEST WINNER!

The next night at dinner, which was mostly beans because Aunt Sally had been to the market, the children said, "Tell us a story."

"What kind of a story?" asked Aunt Sally.

"Another ghost story," said Melissa.

"Yeah, more about trolls," said Amanda.

Aunt Sally looked at Pee Wee and shook her head. "Speaking of ghosts, what are you going to be for Halloween?"

"I wish you could be here for Halloween," said Amanda. "I bet you could think of good ways to scare the trick-or-treaters."

"I never scare trick-or-treaters," said Aunt Sally. "I consider it my job to be the scaree, not the scarer. Have you got your fireworks yet?"

"Fireworks?" said Amanda.

"For Halloween?" said Pee Wee.

"They don't do that here?" asked Aunt Sally. "Huh!"

"We have fireworks on the Fourth of July," said Amanda.

"So do we, on our country's birthday, July first," said Aunt Sally. "Halloween fireworks are something else. Everyone buys their own. Families build bonfires, set off hordes of whizzers and bangers all through the night, if they can afford them. Fireworks are expensive. We never had any money for them, so we would sniff out someone else's display. Sometimes people would go to the beach and set them off over the ocean, and sometimes you'd find a group gathered in a park. What are you going to be for Halloween, Frank?"

"An ugly stepsister," said Frank, sighing.

"An ugly stepsister?" said Aunt Sally.

"We're going as the ugly stepmother, that's me, and the two ugly stepsisters from *Cinderella*," said Melissa.

"Aren't you going to show me your costumes?" asked Aunt Sally.

"We haven't exactly put them together yet," said Amanda. "There aren't enough things in the dress-up clothes box. I'll show you the fairy-tale book. How we *want* them to look."

Amanda ran upstairs, got her book, and opened it to *Cinderella*.

"Hmm," said Aunt Sally, eyeing it critically, "That shouldn't be too hard to do. I can go material-shopping tomorrow. I am having trouble finding ways to fill my days until you get home from school. Let me do a sketch. Got any paper?"

When Amanda brought paper, Aunt Sally with a few deft strokes drew a wonderful dress for the stepmother. Then she looked at Amanda and drew an elaborate dress for her. "Now, Frank, a dress for you?"

"I want to be a ghost," said Pee Wee.

"Hush," said Amanda.

"Shut up," said Melissa.

"Such language," said Aunt Sally.

"They won't let me trick-or-treat with them unless I put on a dress," said Pee Wee.

"Pee Wee!" said Amanda.

"All right for you," said Melissa.

"Girls, girls," said Aunt Sally. "Here, Frank, I'll draw you a special ghost costume. We can get some fluorescent tape and do glow-in-the dark designs."

Amanda glared at Pee Wee. Melissa glared at Pee Wee.

Pee Wee sighed. "Just draw me a dress," he muttered.

"I'll try to make it a particularly masculine dress, Frank," said Aunt Sally. "More beans, anyone?"

Everyone was full, so Aunt Sally started to clean the kitchen and sent Pee Wee upstairs to get ready for bed.

"You never told us a story," said Amanda, as she helped Aunt Sally load the dishwasher.

"So I didn't. Well, let me get Frank settled for the night first."

When Frank had gone to sleep, Aunt Sally came in and sat in the rocker.

"Where did you learn to draw like that?" asked Melissa.

"I didn't really learn, it's just something I could always do. It was a good thing, too, because when I was a child I thought it was the only thing I could do that was special. I wasn't a particularly beautiful or brilliant child. I couldn't play the violin like John, I wasn't saintly like Lyla, I wasn't wildly daring like Edward, and I wasn't the baby in the family like Robbie. Until I learned I could draw, I was a complete washout as an exceptional child. I found out I could draw when I was in the third grade. Every year the school had an earthquake safety poster competition. You had to draw a poster depicting some aspect of earthquake safety. I did a rather nifty poster, I must say, and it won. I was so proud. They hung it right by the school office, with a big blue ribbon on it. The whole family came to the school to see it. Grandpa Willie bought ice cream for dessert that night, and my, wasn't I Queen of the May. I won the next year and the year after that. Then the following year Robbie was old enough to enter. *He* won that year."

"I didn't know Daddy could draw," said Melissa.

"Well, that's the thing," said Aunt Sally. "He can't. Can't now, couldn't then. Nobody seemed to think his winning was quite as incredible as I did. And yet, in a way, I had instigated it."

"What's instigate?" asked Amanda.

"Bring about, now hush," said Melissa.

"I had been lying on my stomach, coloring my poster in front of the fire one evening, when Robbie came by and said, 'I don't like that part over there,' and pointed to a corner of my poster I was particularly proud of. It was a scene where a building had collapsed on a whole third-grade class and many of the little boys were being smushed and squished in a rather bloody way. I thought I was being boldly realistic. The nerve of Robbie, I thought. What did he know about art?

" 'So?' I said to Robbie. 'If you're so smart, why don't you make your own poster?'

"I was only slightly annoyed when he came home with his own poster board. I thought it was pathetic that he thought for one moment he had a chance of winning. I gave him condescending looks of barely concealed amusement whenever he worked on it.

" 'After all,' I said to him, 'it's one thing to make a poster and another to win a contest.'

" 'Do you think I have a chance of being runner-up?' he asked.

" 'No,' I said. 'There aren't runners-up. And even if there were, you would have no chance at all. But I'm glad you've found something to occupy your time.'

"Of course, you know what happened next. After he won the contest, I couldn't look at him without thinking of that conversation and wondering if he thought about it, too. A stone began to rattle around in my stomach.

"The whole family tripped down to the school office, as they had been doing for three years, only this year it was *his* poster hanging with a blue ribbon on it. I didn't think it was fair that he was the baby of the family and had won the poster contest. Then suddenly it occurred to me! But of course! It had all been a hideous mistake. A terrible mix-up. They had declared him the winner when they meant me! After all, mixing up the Andersons wasn't such a bizarre mistake. Not as bizarre as Robbie winning a drawing contest.

"I went to the principal and asked her if perhaps they had meant to name me the winner and gotten my little brother by mistake. She said no. The stone turned into a boulder.

"I waited for Robbie to say something to me like 'And you said I couldn't possibly win.' But he never did. He just smiled a particularly annoying, smug little smile. This made the situation even more insufferable. And, as far as I could tell, no one, *no one*, gave one moment's thought to how bad I might be feeling for losing.

"Grandpa Willie did the usual ice-cream thing, with Robbie gloating the whole evening, and that night Great-uncle Louis gave him a complete drawing set with colored pencils and everything. Naturally, when I had won the contest in years past, he had given me zip. That's when I began to wonder about the trolls.

"I thought about it during school. I thought about it during dinner. I thought about it in the long night hours as I watched the moon travel across my window. In the back of my mind I still thought the whole thing was a mistake and that they had meant to give me the ribbon and had somehow mixed us up but now it was too late to do anything about it. Everyone had moved on to other glories. Except for Robbie and me.

"Robbie clutched this poster-contest business to him like an old blankie and every day he would ask me some insensitive question like 'Will they give me back my poster when they are done with it?' or 'Where do you think I should keep my blue ribbon when I take it home?' Questions that I was sure he knew would twist the knife. I thought he was so selfishly happy that he didn't care how it affected me, or maybe he knew very well how it affected me and was enjoying every moment of my misery. I was too proud to tell him I didn't ever want to hear another word about the poster contest, so every day he asked another question, and every day I thought, if he doesn't drop this soon, I'm going to investigate the existence of the trolls. The questions kept coming: 'Do you think I'll win again next year? Do you think I ought to experiment with different colors? Maybe make it only two colors? Maybe there are other poster contests I could enter.'

" 'So,' I said one day when Edward and John and I were scrambling over boulders down by the sea, sticking our fingers in anemones and catching crabs. 'So, you think there are really trolls down here among the rocks?'

" 'Naw,' said John. He wouldn't stick his fingers in anything any more, not even anemones, but he held the bucket for us to put the crabs in. 'Just one of Great-uncle Louis's weird notions.'

" 'Suppose there are, though,' I said.

" 'Well, suppose there are?' said Uncle Edward.

" 'Don't you want to find out for sure?' I suggested, not looking at them, but scooping up crabs.

" 'How?' asked Edward.

" 'We need some bait. Something to leave on the beach to see if the trolls will get it,' I said.

" 'Are you suggesting we take Tibby down to the beach and see if the trolls will come by?' scoffed John.

" 'Oh no!' I said. 'I'd never do that to Tibby. I was thinking of someone we don't like, such as, um, Robbie.'

"John and Edward just looked at me, but they didn't say anything.

" 'Just an experiment,' I said. 'We'd get him back.'

" 'Oh, brother,' said John. 'You've really slipped your trolley.'

"Edward still didn't say anything, just looked at me. Then we went back to lifting up rocks and catching the scuttling crabs, and none of us mentioned it again."

"You didn't give Daddy to the trolls, though," said Melissa. "Did you?"

"Because he's here now. So you must have decided not to," said Amanda.

"Or there's no such thing as trolls!" said Melissa suddenly with relief.

"Yes, that's it! The whole thing was made up," said Amanda.

Both girls had the covers pulled up to their chins.

"Oh, gosh," said Aunt Sally, looking at her watch. "It's nine o'clock. Lights out!"

AUNT HATTIE'S MIRACLE!

"So," said Melissa on the way home from school with Amanda and Pee Wee. "Tonight's Friday night. We can stay up as late as we want. We'll *make* Aunt Sally finish the story of the trolls."

"What story?" asked Pee Wee.

"Never mind," said Amanda.

"You're too young," said Melissa. "You'll be in bed before she tells us."

"No, I won't," said Pee Wee. "It's Friday night and I can stay up as late as I want."

"*We* can stay up as late as *we* want," said Melissa. "*You* get to stay up an extra half hour and that's all."

The children climbed up the porch steps and threw open the front door. Aunt Sally was peering in the hall mirror, doing something to her eye.

"What's that?" asked Amanda, standing on tippy-toe to see better.

"Eyelash curler," said Aunt Sally. She handed Amanda the instrument. It looked like a pair of scissors but it had two bands that clamped together on the end.

"Cool," said Amanda.

"Awesome," said Melissa. "Can we curl our eyelashes?"

"That would be good for picking up bugs," said Pee Wee.

"I believe you're right, Frank," said Aunt Sally.

"Why would you care about curling your eyelashes?" asked Pee Wee. "You never see anyone. You just sit in the house all day waiting for us to get home."

"Just sit in the house all day, do I?" asked Aunt Sally. "Just sit around? Ha. Come take a look."

She led the children into the living room, where the sewing machine was set up. There, on the dining-room table, was a satin dress with frills and layers. Next to it were two velvet green dresses, one Amanda's size and one Pee Wee's.

The girls gave squeals of pleasure and ran for their costumes. Frank eyed his with wary disgust. When they had been tried on and adjustments made with pins, Aunt Sally said, "I can finish them over the weekend. So, no reason to curl my eyelashes, is there? I walked all the way downtown just to get that fabric, I will have you know."

"Oh, thank you, thank you," said Melissa and Amanda.

"Your eyelashes look pretty straight to me," said Pee Wee.

"That's the point," said Melissa. "They're straight, so you have to curl them."

"Why?" asked Pee Wee.

"In case you meet someone you know in town," said Amanda.

"She doesn't know anyone, so what does she care?" asked Pee Wee.

"I might be like your Great-aunt Hattie. I might meet a mysterious man," said Aunt Sally through a mouthful of pins.

"Great-aunt Hattie?" asked Amanda.

"You don't know about her either? Huh," said Aunt Sally in disgust. "What's the use of having a family history if no one ever passes it down? Come on into the kitchen. I can't do any more sewing today. Come have a snack and I'll draw you pictures. It's time you saw what your relatives looked like."

The children put the cookie jar in the middle of the kitchen table and poured themselves milk. Aunt Sally made herself a cup of tea and got some paper.

"Now," she said. Then she didn't say anything, just sketched for a while. When she was done, the children crowded around the picture. They saw a pebbly beach and an ocean. Two children stood on a path. "That's John and Edward," said Aunt Sally. "And that's me and Lyla."

"Was she a fat little girl?" asked Amanda in amazement, because now Aunt Lyla was as lean as a bean.

"No, not that one, that one was Fat Little Mean Girl. I'll tell you about her someday. The one next to me is Lyla. And that's your daddy."

"Hey, he looks like me," said Pee Wee.

"Yes, he did, Frank. Although he wasn't as devastatingly handsome. Now, over here is your Grandma Evelyn and your Grandpa Willie."

"Grandpa was handsome," said Melissa.

"Grandpa was very distinguished. And this wild-looking hulk of a gent was Great-uncle Louis."

"How come you put him hanging from that tall, tall tree by his knees?" asked Amanda.

"Artistic license. That lady in all the chiffon layers is your Great-aunt Hattie."

"Who's the man on the rocks, the tiny beautiful one?" asked Pee Wee.

"Men can't be beautiful, Pee Wee," said Amanda scathingly.

"Oh, I wouldn't say that," said Aunt Sally. "In fact, beautiful is exactly what that man was. He was the most beautiful man I ever saw before or since. He was small and elfin, with a shock of white hair and a lovely long thin nose and the nicest, kindest, deepest blue eyes I've ever seen. He was so beautiful he was breathtaking. He was so beautiful that even though I was only eleven and he must have been in his seventies I think I was a little in love with him. He was in love with your Great-aunt Hattie. And if it hadn't been for him she might have lived the rest of her life in a kind of stupor."

"Who was he?" asked Melissa.

"What are those two things on the path?" asked Pee Wee, still studying the picture. "They look like gravestones."

"That's what they are, Frank. Those are the gravestones of Hattie's husband, Frank, whom I suspect you were named after, and her daughter, Caroline. That was a horrible story. Your Great-aunt Hattie married late. Everyone said that she was going to be an old maid. She was a not particularly good-looking schoolteacher with a sour disposition and no use for men. She met Frank when she was almost past childbearing years and fell madly in love. They married and bought a cabin in the woods. Frank had a job at the mill and she quit teaching school. When she gave birth to Caroline long past the point anyone thought a lady should be having babies, she was the happiest woman alive. I enjoyed Aunt Hattie myself. She said exactly what she thought, which didn't make her too popular with lots of folks, but I always thought she didn't care about anything at all except Frank and Caroline.

"After the baby came, Frank wanted to upgrade the cabin. It was pretty primitive and he wanted to modernize it and put electricity in. Hattie didn't want to. She didn't think they could afford it yet, and she wanted to save up money so they could send Caroline away to college someday. Mostly girls in town married millworkers and had babies, but Hattie wanted more for Caroline, and she knew that meant a financial escape route. Frank thought the sun rose and set on Hattie, so he opened a bank account for Caroline, and that's where their money went. Hattie was perfectly content, for Caroline's sake, to live in a cabin without electricity or an indoor toilet. Of course, I think eventually, for Caroline's sake, they would have had to *get* an indoor toilet, because, Lord knows, children will latch on to anything to tease another child, and an outhouse would provide the kids in town with plenty of ammunition. But eventually never came. One Saturday Aunt Hattie visited your Grandma Evelyn for tea, and when she got home she found her cabin ablaze. Frank had gone to sleep with baby Caroline on the bed beside him. A lit candle on the bedside table had tipped and set the bedclothes on fire. Frank and Caroline had burned up before they even woke."

"That's *terrible!*" said Amanda.

"Don't you ever tell nice stories?" said Melissa.

"Were they dead?" asked Pee Wee.

"Well, yes, Frank, they were," said Aunt Sally. "A lot of folks said it was Hattie's fault for not getting the electricity in. That was probably because Frank was a whole lot better liked than Hattie. As much as people felt bad about Frank and baby Caroline, I think they were secretly pleased to find a reason to denounce Aunt Hattie, who had always been so sharp-tongued and, worse, had never had any use for them. Grandma Evelyn thought it would kill Hattie, or she'd kill herself, one or the other. We none of us expected her to survive, but she did. She went back to teaching and got herself a room in a boardinghouse in town. Weekends she would stay with us and never talk to anyone but just spend long hours walking the beach. I don't mean she did that for a few months, I mean she did that *year after year.*"

"How did she and Great-uncle Louis get along?" asked Pee Wee. "Did he make her eat her fiddleheads?"

"Well, that's the thing," said Aunt Sally. "No one noticed her after a while. She went around ghostlike. She was like a cat, you know, that lives with you but sort of has a life of its own. Then one day she had the gravestones of Caroline and Frank moved from the little cemetery in town to the path down to the ocean. I guess she wanted to be with them on weekends. You can imagine the kind of talk that started. I think she would have been removed from her teaching post, but she was a good teacher and she wasn't vague or strange at all in the classroom, so nobody could come up with any objections that would stick. And, after all, lots of folks went to the graveyard to visit their dead. Oh, hey, look at the time. I better clean up the mess here and start to make supper. Not that you are going to eat anything after all those cookies. But your mother has written 'six o'clock dinner . . . the kids always like meat loaf.' And look, she has listed everything I need. I know, I'll make a surprise meat loaf."

"What's the surprise?" asked Pee Wee.

"Well, if I told you, dear, there wouldn't *be* a surprise. Now shoo. You all go out and play, right this instant. Run around and work up an appetite."

"But you haven't told us about the mysterious man," said Amanda.

"I'll tell you later, after supper," said Aunt Sally. "I haven't got the mental wherewithal to tell stories and cook at the same time. Good lord, some mornings it's all I can do to get my eyeliner on straight, and here you expect me to be a cross between Julia Child and Scheherazade."

"Who's Julia Child?" asked Amanda.

"Great chef," said Melissa.

"Who's Scheherazade?" asked Amanda.

"Great storyteller. Now shhh," said Melissa.

"Go on, shoo," said Aunt Sally.

The children shooed until Aunt Sally called them for dinner. Aunt Sally gave everyone what had become their usual pile of green beans. Melissa picked one up and peeled off its skin. Pee Wee built a fort out of his and ate it log by log.

"Frank," said Aunt Sally, preparing to serve him a slice of meat loaf, "would you like an end, middle, or semi-middle? Every part of the meat loaf has a different surprise."

"Okay, I'll have a middle" said Pee Wee.

"You can't have *a* middle," said Amanda. "You can only have *the* middle. Nothing has more than one middle."

"I believe," said Aunt Sally, putting the middle piece on Pee Wee's plate, "that Frank meant *a* middle *slice*. The middle is a large area and Frank wanted *a* piece of it. Is that what you meant, Frank?"

"Oh, cool, an olive," said Pee Wee, who was already poking through his slice, looking for possibly more interesting surprises and paying no attention to the constructive criticism of his older sister.

"Amanda, what would you like?" asked Aunt Sally.

"Give me a semi-middle," said Amanda. "Please."

"Okey-doke. And Melissa?"

"An end," said Melissa. She took her plate and stared at it. "A hard-boiled egg?"

"Surprise!" shouted Aunt Sally.

"I got a cooked baby carrot in mine," said Amanda.

"Isn't this fun?" said Aunt Sally. "Okay, someone select a piece for me, since I already know where everything is."

"Take the other end," said Melissa. "I hope you don't get an egg, too."

"Nope," said Aunt Sally, putting the end piece on her plate. "A smoked oyster. I had to open a whole tin of them to get one for the meat loaf, so remind me to make smoked-oyster dip to have with potato chips tomorrow."

"Ugh," said Pee Wee.

"Oh no, Frank, oysters are delicious. Have you ever tried them?"

"No, that's grownup food," said Pee Wee.

"Nonsense. Your aunts and uncles when they were young used to go down to the rocks and harvest oysters. Grandma Evelyn would fry them and we'd put them on French bread and have oyster sandwiches. Mmmm, now that's comfort food. It was because of oysters that we found Aunt Hattie meeting the mysterious man. As I said before, weekends she'd stay with us and walk the beaches. After two years of this, we were pretty accustomed to her wraithlike comings and goings."

"What's wraithlike?" asked Amanda.

"Like a ghost. Shhh," said Melissa.

"One day she came back from the beach with a basket full of oysters. I'd never seen her do that before. It intrigued me. In our quiet little world without toys or television, something like Aunt Hattie's *sudden oystering* was a big event. I told Edward and John and we decided to follow her down to the beach the next morning. The tide was out and the shore glittered like diamonds. Standing on the path going down to the beach was the mysterious man. I swear, *he* glittered. It was the first time any of us had seen him. Lots of people came down to the beach, but he stood out. You ever notice how certain people have something that just draws your eyes to them? Well, he had it in spades. We crouched in the bushes and I watched him, somewhat awestruck and drooling, I must admit. Aunt Hattie began to walk slowly down the beach, and the man took off his black billy boots. He was wearing beautiful khaki pants that he had rolled up at the ankle. He had fine ankles and he walked with a slow, exquisite pleasure through the shallow water, leaving his boots on shore. As he walked down one side of the beach, Aunt

Hattie walked down the other. Then they reversed it. Finally, she stopped and began slowly prying oysters off rocks, but I could see her peeking at him whenever she dared. I knew there was something different about his clothes. They weren't like the pants men in town wore, or like the ones my father wore to the mill. Those khakis, I realize now, were expensive and beautifully cut. I sensed this then and that made it all the more exciting to see them being worn so carelessly through the sand."

"What are khakis?" asked Amanda.

"You know, a kind of brown pants," said Melissa.

"What's beautiful about brown pants?" asked Pee Wee. "I wear brown pants all the time."

"You don't wear beautifully cut brown pants," said Melissa.

"If I ever cut my pants, Mom would be mad," said Pee Wee.

"No, beautifully cut means that they were, well, shaped nicely," said Aunt Sally.

"I don't think that's anything to get so excited about," said Pee Wee.

"If they want to get excited over some nicely shaped brown pants, they can," said Amanda. "This is your great-aunt we're talking about. Show a little respect."

"I am," said Pee Wee. "I just said that I think it's stupid getting all excited over a certain kind of pants. So what if he had brown pants?"

"Will you please ignore him and go on?" said Melissa.

"I'm always happy to get Frank's take on things. Do you have anything else you'd like to share on the subject, Frank?"

Frank shook his head regally. It wasn't often his opinion was valued. He gestured silently that she should continue the story. Melissa threw a bean at him.

"Ahem!" Aunt Sally cleared her throat, anxious to get on before a bean war erupted. "He was tiny and had lovely bones, like a bird or something."

"I don't think birds have lovely bones," said Pee Wee, who began to believe his opinion was wanted on everything. "Can I have more meat loaf?"

"Certainly, Frank," said Aunt Sally, getting up and putting a piece on his plate.

"Oh, yuk," said Pee Wee. "This piece has broccoli in it."

"Another surprise!" said Aunt Sally. "Well, maybe birds don't have lovely bones. I don't know how to describe it. But he sure had lovely ankles."

"How can a man have lovely ankles? I think this is a stupid story," said Pee Wee.

"Pee Wee, that's rude," said Melissa.

"Yeah," said Amanda.

"If everyone's finished, I'll get dessert," said Aunt Sally.

"Wait a second, you have to finish the story," said Melissa.

"Let's all clear the table and I'll cut the cake and tell you the rest of it."

When the dishes were in the dishwasher and everyone had

slices of lemon cake in front of them, Aunt Sally continued. "I went down to the beach every weekend to watch Aunt Hattie and this gentleman. I'm afraid the boys agreed with you about the fascination of lovely ankles, Frank, so after the first spying expedition they found more interesting things to do. Aunt Hattie and the mysterious man were so aware of each other that they might as well have been two people alone in a small room. I don't think either one of them took notice of the ocean anymore. I tried to breathe quietly for fear any noise would break the spell.

"One weekend I heard Grandma Evelyn say to Aunt Lyla, who was most like her confidante, 'Have you noticed how Aunt Hattie seems happier lately? And how maybe finally after all these years she's getting over things?' That's how Grandma Evelyn always referred to it: 'getting over things,' 'we are waiting for Hattie to get over things,' 'Hattie will buy a house when she gets over things,' 'Hattie will go back to church when she gets over things,' 'Hattie will speak to us at dinner when she gets over things.'

"I was always a little jealous of Grandma Evelyn's relationship with Aunt Lyla and I always thought they thought I was too much a harum-scarum tomboy to be included in these tête-à-têtes. So I marched in on this discussion and said importantly that I knew why Aunt Hattie was happier and I led them down to the beach, where the atmosphere was, as usual, so thick you felt your own heart hammer faster sympathetically.

"Grandma Evelyn and Lyla watched Aunt Hattie picking the oysters slowly off the rocks one by one and the gentleman pulling his ankles slowly through the cold clear water, and Grandma Evelyn said, 'Well, I certainly never saw him before. Who is that man, Lyla?' But Lyla didn't know. Grandma Evelyn began to make it her business to find out. I'd catch her rocking with Lyla on the porch, saying things like, 'Well, he's not been staying at Lillian's B and B, and Janet at the market says he hasn't been in to buy anything.' They didn't exactly keep all this a secret from me, but they didn't go out of their way to confide in me either."

"That's kind of rotten," said Amanda.

"Yeah," said Melissa. "You were the one who showed them the man to begin with."

"Oh well, this isn't my story anyhow. Hattie became more and more radiant on weekends, and she even started speaking at the dinner table. This changed the dynamics of dinnertime for a while. Great-uncle Louis was used to dominating the conversation with what us kids called his State of the Union address. Grandma Evelyn deferred to whoever was speaking, Grandpa Willie was a silent eater for the most part. We kids just wanted to eat and get out of there mostly, although we did hope Edward would take a dislike to another vegetable, because there's nothing like watching someone drop out of a third-floor window, but he never did. Great-uncle Louis had the floor unchallenged, until Hattie started to speak, and when she spoke, it turned out that she thought Great-uncle Louis was an old windbag. This caused some considerable friction at the table, which all us children enjoyed immensely, with the possible exception of Lyla, the sainted. When Hattie snorted and called Great-uncle Louis less a man than an excuse to keep up a mustache, Grandma Evelyn sighed and said, 'We're so glad you're feeling better, Hattie.'

"After dinner, as I cleared the table, I caught Grandma Evelyn saying to Lyla, 'Isn't it a shame that Hattie is too shy to speak to him and he's too shy to speak to her. I have pretty much made up my mind to go down to the beach and say something to him. Maybe I can get him talking to me and then draw her into the conversation in a natural way.'

"I thought this was the dumbest idea I had ever heard. I mean, when had Aunt Hattie ever been shy? If they were enjoying being aware of each other without speaking, why spoil it? I marched over and said this, but of course no one paid any attention to me because I was just an eleven-year-old tomboy."

"I know how you felt," said Pee Wee.

"How would you know?" said Amanda. "You're not eleven."

"You're only six," said Melissa. "And you don't know anything."

"Now hush," said Amanda.

"The next Saturday, after Hattie had left for the beach, Grandma and Lyla and I followed her down. Grandma Evelyn was intent on speaking to the mysterious gentleman. We were all nervous—he was so beautiful and sparkling. I wondered if his voice would be beautiful and sparkling, too. I was probably the most nervous, since I had watched him the longest. I wondered if talking to him would be like pricking a balloon with a pin and we'd see all the pretty air blow away."

"Pretty air?" said Pee Wee. "How can air be pretty?"

"It's a metaphor," said Melissa.

"What's a metaphor?" asked Amanda.

"It's something that's like something else," said Melissa.

"I want some more cake," said Pee Wee.

Aunt Sally cut more cake for everyone.

"I was sweating," she continued. "I remember clearly cold damp beads coming down my shirt, because I realized I was going to meet the mysterious man. I wanted to and I didn't. We got down to the beach and saw Aunt Hattie walking kind of distractedly. She had a self-conscious look as she shot surreptitious glances toward the various paths which the mysterious man might take down to the beach. Then she walked back. We stayed undetected on the path. For the first time the mysterious man was missing. We waited, but he never came, so we left Aunt Hattie walking back and forth until finally she took off her shoes, lifted her skirt, and dragged her ankles slowly through the waves. We came down the next day, but he wasn't there. Then the weekend was over and we had to wait for the next one. He never showed up the following weekend or the one after that or the one after that. He was gone."

"I don't understand," said Melissa. "How could he have just left? Wasn't he in love with Aunt Hattie?"

"Of course he was in love with Aunt Hattie. We all knew he was in love with Aunt Hattie."

"Well, what happened to him? Who was he? There's more to the story, isn't there?" asked Amanda.

"Nope, that's it," said Aunt Sally.

Amanda and Melissa stared at her.

"You better give us some more cake," said Melissa. "That's the most disappointing story I ever heard. Was Aunt Hattie devastated? Did she go back to not speaking to anyone?"

"No, that's the funny thing of it. You'd think such a crushing blow would have been the final straw in what was turning out to be a pretty rotten life, but instead she perked up and, without ever giving any reason for her change of behavior, she did, as Grandma Evelyn kept predicting, get over things. She bought a house, joined some clubs, went back to church, took an interest in life, started speaking her mind and devil take the hindermost, and she stopped spending the weekend with us. She never returned to the beach."

"It's kind of, well, a disappointing end, isn't it?" said Amanda. "I mean, what was the point?"

"It was certainly anticlimactic," said Aunt Sally. "But now when I ponder the whole thing as a grownup I think of it more as Aunt Hattie's miracle. I think when Frank and Caroline died, something in Hattie died, too. It must take all your energy just to put one foot in front of the other when you're walking around dead. Then, when this mysterious man appeared on the beach, he saw something alive in her, and when she saw him, she saw it, too, and she clung to that little piece of life even after he disappeared, like someone desperately hanging on to a branch over a raging river, hanging on and hanging on and hanging on until they can finally pull themselves to shore."

"But what happened to the mysterious man?" asked Amanda.

"Maybe he was her guardian angel," said Melissa. "And he appeared just long enough to get her back on track."

"Maybe he met with a tragic accident going down to the beach that morning," said Amanda.

"Maybe a rogue wave got him," said Pee Wee.

"Yes," said Melissa. "Fifteen minutes before Great-aunt Hattie came down to the beach."

"Why fifteen?" said Pee Wee.

"Oh, for heavens sake's, Pee Wee," said Melissa. "It's just a number. How many minutes do *you* think it was?"

"I don't know. I just wondered how come you said exactly fifteen?" said Pee Wee.

"Maybe he was there on vacation but he had to go home," said Amanda.

"He would have finally spoken to her," said Melissa. "He would have asked her to come with him."

"Maybe his billy boots sprung leaks and he sank," said Pee Wee, giggling.

"That is exactly what your Aunt Lyla and Grandma Evelyn and I did for months afterwards. We'd sit on the porch and drink lemonade and rock in the rockers and say things like, 'Maybe he was hiking down from a cabin he'd just bought and got lost and is still wandering the woods.' 'Maybe he went away to buy an engagement ring and when he got back Aunt Hattie wasn't taking her beach walks anymore.' 'Maybe he died suddenly, leaving no identification or next of kin.' 'Maybe he came down with a contagious disease and went away to be cured.' And on and on and on. After I grew up, I'd sometimes phone your grandma and the conversation would begin, 'Maybe he ran out of those perfectly cut khaki pants and was waiting for a new shipment.' And Grandma Evelyn would say, 'Maybe he took the ferry to Vancouver to buy some and fell off the side and no one noticed.' "

"Do you and Aunt Lyla still start phone conversations that way?" asked Amanda. Grandma Evelyn had been dead for many years now.

"Lyla and I don't have phone conversations. Well, Pee Wee, I see we've kept you up pretty late and you didn't even think much of the story, now, did you?"

"I like stories with lots of things happening better," said Pee Wee. "Don't you have any more stories like the clam-bite one or maybe one where someone gets eaten by a bear?"

"Pee Wee!" said Amanda.

"Gross!" said Melissa. "Serves you right if we tell you about the trolls."

"Ixnay, ixnay," said Aunt Sally. "Come on and brush your teeth, Frank. At least you know where your name came from."

"Why don't you ever talk to Lyla on the phone?" asked Amanda.

"Oh, this whole Aunt Hattie thing was before the you-know-whats," said Aunt Sally.

"You have to finish that story," said Melissa.

"Yeah," said Amanda.

"Tell me, too," said Pee Wee. "And put in someone being eaten by a bear."

"Not tonight," said Aunt Sally. "There's such a thing as being talked out." She got up, put the cake plates in the dishwasher, and paused, bent over the open dish rack. "I guess he must be dead by now, the mysterious man. But you can't help when someone just disappears, always, always thinking of him. I'm sure Aunt Hattie did. Right until she died. And maybe that's what he wanted."

PINBALL!

Saturday Melissa and Amanda went to play at friends' houses and Pee Wee was at soccer all day. At four everyone convened at the Andersons'. It was one of those perfectly glorious October days when the trees are all tipped with gold, the sun smiles on everything, and the earth is alive with a last sparkle of energy before winter kills it.

"It's Saturday night and I'm tired of my own cooking," said Aunt Sally. "You got any place to eat in this town?"

"There's Murray's," said Pee Wee.

"Oh, Pee Wee," said Melissa. "Murray's is so small-town and greasy."

"She means someplace nice like McDonald's," said Amanda.

"Murray's has booths and a jukebox and a pinball machine," said Pee Wee.

"Sounds perfect to me. Can we walk, do you think?" asked Aunt Sally. "Or should I get us a cab?"

"I want to walk," said Melissa. "It gives you shapely legs."

"Who cares about shapely legs?" said Pee Wee. "I want to go in a cab. We never get to go in cabs. And I want to sit on the jump seat."

"My goodness, do they still have cabs like that here?" said Aunt Sally. "That's almost too good to pass up. On the other hand, if we take a cab right now, we'll be there way too early to eat. Let's walk there and take a cab home."

The four of them set out, scuttling leaves along the road, watching squirrels take nuts up trees to hide them.

"How was soccer, Frank?" asked Aunt Sally.

"Okay. Did Daddy used to play soccer?"

"Oh yes. Soccer is very big on the island because you can play year round."

"I thought it rained," said Amanda.

"It does. They play in the rain. Those soccer people are fanatic. If you ask me, they like it better in the rain. Makes them feel like warriors, coming home covered head to foot in mud. Of course, it's not as muddy as bull-moose wrestling. They used to have that every year in the fall. The next question I know will be what is bull-moose wrestling. It's just what it says it is. Men go into the woods and round up a bunch of bull moose and wrestle them to the ground."

"Did Daddy do that?" asked Pee Wee.

"No, but naturally your Great-uncle Louis did. The men used to take their shirts off, cover their silly hairy chests with baby oil, and wrestle those moose."

"I think that's awful," said Melissa. "They should leave those wild moose alone."

"Well, this was before anyone knew animals had rights, dear. Your aunts and uncles and I thought moose wrestling was just plain dumb. And Grandma Evelyn, too, though she wouldn't come right out and say it. That would have been encouraging us to disrespect Great-uncle Louis. During bull-moose wrestling season Great-uncle Louis would come home every evening simply covered in mud, with a pile of muddy clothes for Grandma Evelyn to wash. It tried her patience sorely. Instead of taking his weekly Saturday bath, Great-uncle Louis had to bathe every single night. And he had to bathe in rather a hurry, so that he could be changed and downstairs in time for dinner. So he began to invent the perfect way to take an efficient bath. This of course became the subject of his State of the Union address night after weary night.

" 'I know what to do with the soap now, Evelyn,' he would say. 'Are you listening, Edward? Look alive, John. You hold it in the *left* hand to begin with. Have you got that? The *left* hand.'

" 'Not the right, as you might think,' said John, who could be perfectly acid without Great-uncle Louis noticing.

" 'Not the right, John, the *left*. And you run it down the right side of the body, starting at the tip of the right ear.'

" 'Maybe I should be taking notes,' said John, getting up.

" 'Please sit down and eat your dinner, John,' said Grandma Evelyn, sighing. She knew John was being sarcastic and she always lived in mortal fear that Great-uncle Louis would find out and there'd be more people leaping out of third-floor windows.

" 'Now,' said Great-uncle Louis, waving a chicken bone around, 'can you guess what happens when you reach the bottom of your right heel?'

"Lyla always blushed through this whole business. Watching her slowly turn cerise was one of the few pleasures I got out of these long bath lectures."

"What's cerise?" asked Amanda.

"Red. Shhh," said Melissa.

"Great-uncle Louis kept on and on about the art of the fast bath. One night he brought a washtub down and put it right next to the dining-room table, saying, 'Visual aid, Evelyn, visual aid.' Halfway through supper, as he explained the refinements he had made in his bathing technique, he *hopped* into the tub. He left his mashed potatoes and turnips and brisket and leapt in, demonstrating scrubbing technique with his dinner napkin. Lyla was practically apoplectic by that point.

" 'The wonderful thing, Evelyn,' Great-uncle Louis said to Grandma Evelyn, who kept her eyes focused on her plate rather than watch him take a bath with all his clothes on right there in front of us all. 'The wonderful thing is that tomorrow night begins the final championships of the moose-wrestling season and I'll be as muddy as a riverbed in springtime. I can't imagine better circumstances for practicing my technique. I can demonstrate the infinitesimal refinements at dinner.' "

"What's infinitesimal?" asked Amanda.

"Tiny," said Melissa.

"I think something in Grandma Evelyn finally snapped because when we got home from school the next day she informed us children that Grandpa Willie was working a night shift at the mill, so she was taking us out for dinner.

" 'What about Great-uncle Louis?' asked your daddy.

" 'I have left his dinner in the oven with a note,' said Grandma Evelyn. 'Land's sake, can't we eat out once a century?'

"Well, we were flabbergasted. I don't think we could any of us remember Grandma Evelyn ever taking us out to dinner. It simply wasn't done. We were pretty excited as we walked into town. There wasn't a lot of choice of where to eat in those days. There was a burger shack on the beach and a Dairy Queen and the café. We chose the café because we could all sit down, and Grandma Evelyn said she wanted to linger over dinner. That's when I figured out she was trying to avoid Great-uncle Louis and his bath. Anyhow, we got there and sat in two booths right next to each other and started looking at the menu, and your daddy says, 'Hey, look, they got a jukebox and a pinball machine. Mom, can I put a dime in the jukebox?' In those days, you got a song for a dime and three for a quarter. Grandma

Evelyn, who was eyeing the pinball machine, astounded us by opening her purse and passing us a quarter. We had a thoroughly satisfying argument over which three songs to choose and who got to drop in the quarter and push the buttons. We sat back down and returned to our menus and then Grandma Evelyn said, 'Children, before I order, I'm going to take this dime and play the pinball machine. Just once.'

"If you'd told us kids that we were adopted, we wouldn't have been more surprised. Grandma Evelyn was an extremely practical woman. We never had any fripperies in our house."

"What's a frippery?" asked Amanda.

"Beats me," said Melissa.

"Oh, you know, a la-di-da luxury. Not that Grandma Evelyn was cheap. She was as generous as she could be with the money that was around, which was practically none. And not that she didn't take any pleasure in stuff, but the kind of stuff we had pleasure in was library books and walking down to the ocean and trying to figure out what the heck the grownups were up to—pleasures that were free. We would have been surprised if Grandma Evelyn had bought us all a small toy at the drugstore or a new hair ribbon even, but to throw her dime away on *pinball!* And not even pinball for us, but pinball for herself. I guess, when you got down to it, we had never seen Grandma Evelyn do something just for herself. We hung over her shoulder and stared dumbstruck as she dropped in her dime and the machine started whizzing. We'd never seen it played before, so we weren't sure what was going on with all the dinging and banging and numbers coming up on the board. Grandma Evelyn flipped flippers and pulled levers and *pounded* the side of the machine. It was worth more than a dime to see that.

" 'I never knew you played pinball,' I said to Grandma Evelyn.

" 'Now, don't you go telling your father about this,' said Grandma Evelyn sternly when she finished a game.

" 'Is that a good score?' asked John.

" 'Not too bad, considering I haven't played in years,' said Grandma Evelyn, looking thoughtfully at the board.

" 'Play again, play again,' said us kids.

" 'Well . . .' said Grandma Evelyn. She rooted through her purse until she found three more dimes. 'Just a couple of times before we order dinner maybe.'

" 'Can we play one game?' asked John.

" 'No,' said Grandma Evelyn. She dropped the dime in and was in her own little world. I don't think she even knew we were there anymore. She played two more times. We were hungry and started edging back to the booths to order. Grandma Evelyn joined us, flushed and smiling. 'I doubled it!' she said triumphantly. We sat down and were about to ask for our cheeseburgers, onion rings, and milk shakes when Grandma Evelyn says to the waitress, 'Miss, could you give me some dimes for these?' She handed the waitress *two dollars*.

" 'Sure thing,' said the waitress. 'You want to order now?'

" 'Maybe a bit later,' said Grandma Evelyn. She began by letting each of us kids play one game and then she took back the machine and went at it hammer and tongs. People watched her from their booths as they ate their dinners. She gripped the machine with total concentration, never even noticing when Edward, who had gotten bored, went to do one of his jop ratings."

"What's that?" asked Amanda.

"Edward's hobby in those days was rating public bathrooms. He recorded everything in a notebook and called it his jop ratings. We never knew what jop stood for or meant. He knew all the gas-station bathrooms and on Saturdays would go into town, ask for the key, and update the ratings. He kept the notebook in his back pocket and, no matter where we went, was forever delaying us by finding and inspecting the washroom. I don't know what he rated, the towels and toilets for cleanliness and stuff, I guess. It always seemed to take him an eternity. He'd come out making check marks and writing down numbers and announce, 'A point five one one o,' or something, and we'd all go 'Oh, good, Edward, that relieves our minds considerably,' or something equally sarcastic. As a family goes, we could be quite sarcastic, at least when Grandma Evelyn didn't put a lid on it. Anyhow, Edward goes off happy as a pig in a puddle, because he has a new bathroom to rate. Grandma Evelyn keeps changing bills into dimes, and we're all getting hungrier and hungrier, wondering just how much longer she plans to keep this up before we can order. I begin to worry privately that she might be spending our dinner money; bills are flying out of her purse like confetti. Just as I am thinking that it is taking Edward much too long to rate the bathroom, the waitress comes up and taps Grandma Evelyn on the shoulder and says, 'Excuse me, ma'am, but do you have a son named Edward?'

" 'Umm hmmm,' says Grandma Evelyn, who can't be bothered with offspring right now.

" 'Well, he seems to be trapped in the bathroom.'

" 'Come on! Come on! Come on!' says Grandma Evelyn, pounding the machine and flipping flippers.

" 'Ma'am, *he can't get out,*' says the waitress.

" 'No, no, he's just rating it. He'll come out when he's ready,' says Grandma Evelyn. 'Bingo! Bingo!' She's been yelling this excitedly every time the ball does what she wants.

" 'No, he *can't,* apparently. He's been yelling through the door for the last half hour. It seems he locked the door, then stuck his hand up the towel machine, and now he can't get his hand out.'

" 'Well, unlock the door!' screamed Grandma Evelyn, who wasn't paying much attention and was in such a frenzy that she was screaming everything now.

" 'We can't! We don't have a key!' screamed the waitress back.

" 'What do you mean, you don't have a key? How do you usually get people out when they've trapped themselves in the towel machine?' yelled Grandma Evelyn, still dropping in dimes and pushing buttons.

" 'The situation has never come up before!' yelled the waitress right back.

" 'Well, for heaven's sake! Pick the lock, take the door off the hinges; must you bother me with every little detail?' screamed Grandma Evelyn.

" 'He seems rather frightened,' said the waitress. 'Wouldn't you like to *talk* to him?'

" 'No, I would not,' said Grandma Evelyn. 'Can't you see I'm on a roll?'

"In the end, they had the fire department in to take down the door, because none of the women working in the café knew how to take off a door hinge. Grandma Evelyn didn't even notice the firemen coming through in their uniforms with equipment and axes. Somewhere in the middle of this rescue operation, she ran out of dimes. She not only ran out of dimes, she ran out of all the money in her purse, so she sat down. It was at this moment that Edward arrived, rather shaken, in the arms of a fireman. We had a volunteer fire department, and the town awarded a medal every year for the bravest act, so the volunteers were always climbing all over each other, trying to outdo one another with unnecessary heroics.

" 'Put me down!' yelled Edward. 'I'm fine!'

" 'Might be smoke damage,' said the fireman.

" 'There wasn't even a fire!' said Edward.

The fireman couldn't refute this, so he finally had to drop Edward, at which point Edward finally did suffer a casualty, landing with a thud on his tailbone, which became tremendously bruised and bothered him for years afterwards.

" 'How long did you plan to abandon me there?' said Edward, who was simply furious at us all.

"Before we could answer, the waitress returned and said icily to us, 'Would you care to order now?'

"Grandma Evelyn looked in her purse, said, 'Perhaps another time,' and shepherded us outside, where she explained she had spent all her money on pinball. We trudged the long way home in darkness, with everyone's stomach growling.

" 'Just what were you doing with your hand up the towel machine anyway, Edward?' asked Grandma Evelyn with mild curiosity.

" 'I was trying to ascertain just how many towels were left. It's part of my rating,' said Edward.

" 'Well, if that isn't stupid,' said Robbie.

" 'I'll have you know I *always* check the towel supply, and this is the first time I've been trapped by the machine. It does not bode well for its rating, it does not bode well at all,' added Edward darkly.

"No one asked Grandma Evelyn where our dinner might be coming from that evening. We went wearily into the house and saw by the muddy footprints that Great-uncle Louis had come in, taken his bath, and had his dinner. We could hear his gentle snores floating down from his bedroom. On the kitchen table was a large chocolate moose—first prize in the bull-moose wrestling championships.

" 'Good heavens, he must be completely exhausted to have fallen asleep so soon after dinner,' said Grandma Evelyn, eyeing the chocolate moose. 'All this moose wrestling has tired him out.'

"We sat down at the kitchen table, by tacit agreement broke up the chocolate moose, ate the whole thing, and never to this day mentioned the pinball incident to another soul."

Murray's appeared around the bend. Melissa, Amanda, Pee Wee, and Aunt Sally sat down and ordered cheeseburgers and onion rings and milk shakes. When the waitress had set the food before them, they lifted their cheeseburgers and said, "To Grandma Evelyn!"

"To Grandma Evelyn!" said Aunt Sally solemnly. "And may there be pinball in heaven."

MAUD WHO SHOT EIGHTY COUGARS!

All Sunday, the children made the most of Aunt Sally. She finished their Halloween costumes, proved a tireless player of cribbage and I Doubt It, read Mrs. Piggle-Wiggle stories out loud, using just the right expression, and never put a lid on the cookie jar. She was, all in all, the most satisfactory grownup the children had ever known. At dinnertime, as she took a fragrant pot roast and the ubiquitous green beans off the stove, the children sighed.

"I can't believe you have to go tomorrow," said Melissa, stretching and yawning in a Sunday-evening way.

"Yeah, you have to tell us at least one more story," said Amanda.

"You still have to finish the troll story," said Melissa.

"Ixnay, ixnay," said Aunt Sally, eyeing Pee Wee.

"Tell us a story at dinner," said Amanda.

"Tell us something about our relatives," said Melissa.

"Tell us a scary story with cougars and bears," said Pee Wee.

"All right," said Aunt Sally, sitting down and pushing pot roast around her plate reflectively. "Get me that picture I drew for you of our family."

Melissa fetched it and Aunt Sally got to work sketching again. She drew a big old gingerbready house with towers and a porch on a hill. On the porch she put a short older woman leaning over the railing with a shotgun in her hand and a cougar skin hung next to her.

"There," she said, and passed it round.

"Who's that?" asked Pee Wee.

"That's Maud who shot eighty cougars. Maud lived on a hill up the road about a half mile from us in one of those big, mysterious Gothic houses you always want to see the inside of. We knew her slightly, enough to say hello if we ran into her in the grocery store or wave to her on her porch if we walked past, but we didn't know much about her. We didn't know if she had ever been married or how she got her money. We thought she must be rich because of the huge, expensive house she rattled around in all alone. Sometimes we wondered what she did all day, but mostly she was a fixture."

"What's that?" asked Pee Wee.

"What I mean is that when I was a child I fixed my position in the universe by a few things surrounding me that seemed forever and unchanging. There was the beach, the forest,

Cooter's Island, the Hoffners, and Maud who lived in the house on the hill. It was rumored that she had shot eighty cougars on her property. I never saw a cougar, as I said before, although the woods were full of them. I thought it was strange that I went into the woods all the time and never saw a single one and she had shot *eighty*.

"There was something I wanted John and Edward to do with me but I thought first we should have a test of courage." Aunt Sally looked meaningfully at Melissa and Amanda. "John and Edward liked the idea of a test of courage. It was John's idea to get out the poster paints and paint strange signs on our faces like natives going into battle.

" 'Now we have to find something daring to do,' said Edward.

" 'Yes,' said John. 'What scary thing is there to do around here?'

" 'We'll step on the gravestones of Frank and Caroline,' I said. Aunt Hattie, when she had moved the gravestones, had put them in the path horizontally like steps. You could hardly read Caroline and Frank's names anymore, so covered with dirt were they. We were always careful never ever to step on the stones but went out of our way to scramble around them. It was one of those strange, contagious superstitions. Edward and John agreed that breaking such a profound taboo would be a good test of courage. We painted our faces with thick yellow lines and painted red arrows on our noses, then we went down the path and stepped right in the middle of the gravestones. We were all terrified for the week that followed. When nothing dreadful happened to us, it was quite a letdown.

" 'We need another test of courage,' I said. It was a Saturday and we were hanging around climbing trees and having stone-skipping contests. 'Let's knock on Maud's door and ask her if she really shot eighty cougars.'

"John and Edward thought this was a fine idea. We decided it would be more daring if we spied on her first. After all, we might as well make a day of it. We walked up the road, climbed the side of the hill to the back of her house, and peeked in all her windows. She had heavy dark old furniture and a lot of gilt-edged mirrors and doilies everywhere. It looked like a museum. John decided we should climb up the porch side to the roof and peek in the second-story windows. We were going from bedroom to bedroom when Maud stuck her head out a window and said, 'Just what do you think you're doing?'

"This was a pretty good question. This was such a good question that Edward almost fell off the roof, trying to think of an answer. He was hanging from a finial when he finally blurted out, 'Did you really shoot eighty cougars on your property?'

" 'Good heavens, is that it?' said Maud, who had opened the window, climbed out on the roof, and was making her way over to Edward. 'Try not to break that finial, boy. It's so hard to get the darned things repaired these days.' "

"What's a finial?" asked Melissa.

"It's this kind of pointed thing they have on old houses. Sort of a decoration. It was really good of Maud to come out on the roof. She was late-middle-age, heading for old, and rather large (cumbersome, not humongous), and one could tell that the roof wasn't her natural habitat. She shuffled unsurely over to Edward, got hold of his belt, and pulled, while he scrambled to get one leg back up over the side. They heaved together until finally he was out of danger. Then we sat there, breathing hard for a few minutes.

" 'Would you like to come in?' asked Maud finally.

"So we climbed rather self-consciously through an upstairs window, went tippy-toeing through a bedroom and on downstairs. I kept nudging the boys and pointing, because there were cougar skins everywhere, over banisters, stretched above fireplaces, and placed as hearth rugs before them.

" 'Did you shoot all these?' asked Edward.

" 'Well, they didn't die of old age,' said Maud.

" 'Wow,' said John. 'Can we see your rifle?'

"Maud brought out an old hunting rifle and we examined it. She showed us some of the other stuffed things she had lying around: an owl, a snake, a bluebird standing on a tree branch. When Maud talked about preserving nature, she didn't mean what most people mean.

" 'Did you shoot this little bluebird?' I couldn't help asking Maud.

" 'Now, honey, I wouldn't do that,' said Maud. 'That'd leave a big old bullet hole. I had to make a wee pillowcase and suffocate the dear. Jeez, I hate having to do that.'

"I decided it was time to go home.

" 'Gotta go,' I said, dragging the boys out the door.

" 'Well, you say hello to your mother,' said Maud. 'And, say, come on back early morning next Saturday if you're not doing anything, and I'll take you on a cougar hunt. Haroo-haroo.'

"John and Edward and I had a bit of a set-to on the way home. The boys wanted to go on the cougar hunt. In fact, they couldn't think of anything they'd rather do. I was having uneasy feelings about Maud.

" 'And what does "haroo-haroo" mean?' I asked.

" 'I dunno,' said John. 'Maybe she didn't mean anything by it.'

" 'Or maybe we heard her wrong. Maybe she said "hello hello," ' said Edward.

" 'Why would she say hello as we were leaving?' I asked. 'I think there's something creepy about her and her dead menagerie.'

" 'That's why it's a test of courage,' persisted Edward. 'If you weren't afraid to go, where would the courage part come in?'

" 'You're not afraid to go,' I said. 'You *want* to go. I can tell.'

" 'I'm shaking in my shoes,' insisted Edward, and set his jaw. When he got that look, there was no use arguing with him.

"Edward worked on me all week until I agreed to go on the cougar hunt. The next Saturday we arrived at Maud's house dressed in green to blend into the forest. Edward wanted to paint our faces yellow and red again, but John and I thought this would attract too much cougar attention. Maud was wearing big rubber boots, baggy green pants, a red-checked hunting jacket, and was carrying a rifle, with a knife at her belt.

" 'If we catch one, can we have the skin?' asked Edward.

" 'It's pretty expensive to have a taxidermist skin it,' said Maud. 'I couldn't keep all eighty that I shot.'

" 'What did you do with the ones you didn't have skinned?' I asked.

" 'I just threw them back into the forest. Let Mother Nature take care of her own, I always say,' said Maud.

" 'Maybe Great-uncle Louis would have the cougar skinned,' whispered Edward to me and John.

" 'Who's going to ask him—*you*? You fiddlehead lover, you,' I muttered.

" 'We could ask Robbie to,' said Edward.

" 'Is this before or after we give him to the trolls?' murmured John. As I said, everyone in our family had a strong sarcastic streak."

"Give him to the whats?" asked Pee Wee.

"Never mind," snapped Melissa.

"Must you know everything?" said Amanda.

Aunt Sally threw Pee Wee a sympathetic look and continued, "We were tromping out pretty far into the woods by now. Nothing but a green canopy overhead, so vast you couldn't see the sky and so dense that when it rained hard only a mist filtered through to us."

"Like the jungle," said Amanda.

"Like the Amazon," said Melissa.

"Like Tarzan," said Pee Wee, and let out a long cry.

"Shut up," said Amanda, covering her ears.

"Such language," said Aunt Sally. "So there we were, walking deeper and deeper and deeper into the woods, and Maud begins to tell us cougar stories, because, as it turns out, Maud has this little obsession with cougar stories."

"What's an obsession?" asked Amanda.

"Keen interest," said Melissa. "Now hush."

"She starts by telling us of a mother and her three kids who are riding horseback on vacation in the interior of British Columbia—the interior is the mainland, not on Vancouver Island, and just what it sounds like, the inside part of the province."

"What's a province?" asked Pee Wee.

"You hush up," said Melissa.

"It's like a state, Pee Wee, like Ohio. Anyhow, they're riding along and a cougar suddenly leaps out of the bush and pulls the youngest son off his horse and onto the ground, where he proceeds to scalp him. The mother screams, leaps off her horse, pulls the cougar off her son, and wrestles with him, meanwhile yelling for her two other children to grab the younger boy, run, and get help. They pick up their younger brother and race through the woods until they come to a road where fortunately there is a man walking with a shotgun, but by the time they bring him back to the site, the cougar has dragged the mother into the bushes and from all accounts is sitting there eating her. Well, we children were horrified. I had always thought that if I met a cougar in the woods I would just yell at it or throw sticks or something until it backed off, but now I suddenly realized great shows of courage such as this mother had performed don't necessarily result in happy endings. At least for the human. I suppose the cougar thought the ending was happy enough.

"I said, 'Doesn't look very cougary today; let's go get some breakfast.'

" 'Now, don't worry, child,' says Maud. 'I'm as scared of cougars as you, but don't forget, we've got this here rifle.' Then she launches into her second cougar story. By this time I am holding Edward's hand, even though he keeps trying to shake me off. It seems there was a man out with his dog and they're hunting ducks. The dog goes off to retrieve a mallard but doesn't come back. So the man calls and calls and finally gets real mad and goes tromping off after his dog. He sees the long grasses by the lake parting, and he thinks it's a dog, but it's not, naturally, since this is Maud's story; it's the cougar who has eaten his dog. He jumps the man and eats him, too. Now John wants to go home. Maud keeps pressing on, telling cougar story after cougar story. None of them end with the cougar getting shot and stuffed, which, judging by all the stuffed cougars you see in town, clearly happens on a regular basis—nope, in Maud's stories, the cougar always wins. Maud rested for a minute on a fallen tree and we thought with relief that she might be turning around for home. Instead, she told a story of a family of twelve who went into the woods and were all found dead and eaten by an entire family of cougars or something. Even Edward wants to go home now. I've pretty much stopped listening to the stories and am trying to recite the alphabet backwards in my head, which is what I do when I don't want to think about something horrible that is happening.

" 'Please, please,' I say to Maud. 'Please, let's forget the whole thing. I don't want to be eaten by a cougar,' when suddenly Maud fires off a shot. 'THERE'S ONE!' she cries, and goes racing down the trail after it.

"There's nothing to do but follow her. We know that it would be sheer folly to turn tail and run back to the house. We'd be easy prey for the cougar, and Maud has the gun. So we jog behind her, with me praying that she's as keen a shot as she seems to be. Pretty soon she points the rifle up a tree and lets off another shot, but nothing drops.

" 'Looks like he got away that time,' she says. 'But you tykes don't worry. He's still out there, like as not circling us, ready to attack from any side at any moment, as soon as we let our guard down. Beef jerky, anyone?'

"Needless to say, none of us felt like a chaw of beef jerky, so

Maud shrugged and had a bite herself, and we continued walking, with Maud jauntily slinging the rifle over her shoulder.

" 'Don't you think you ought to have that thing at the ready?' asked John.

" 'Goodness no, might shoot it off by accident and hit you or Edward or Sally.'

"So we kept going, John and Edward and I craning our necks, looking for the cougar. We took turns suggesting that we head back, but Maud just kept singing this little ditty that went, 'Goin' on a cougar hunt, haroo-haroo.' Finally, when our nerves are stretched about at taut as they'll go, Maud suddenly swings her gun around and lets off a shot. I'm happy to see that she can have the thing cocked and fired in less than a second. A squirrel drops from a tree.

" 'EIGHTY-ONE!' she says exultantly.

"Edward and John and I look at each other. Who is going to say it?

" 'Maud,' I said finally. 'That's a squirrel.'

"I don't think she paid a bit of attention; she just picked up that dead squirrel by its tail and heaved it into the woods.

" 'Can we go home now?' we ask, but Maud is paying no attention. She's walking merrily along, chewing on her beef jerky, carrying the rifle jauntily over one shoulder. We're still not sure if Maud has seen a cougar or not. The fact that she thinks the squirrel she shot was one does not bode well. We are still on the lookout for cougars when she fires again. Something big is racing through the woods toward us. John and Edward and I try to climb on top of each other all at once.

" 'Don't shoot! Don't shoot!' the figure cries, but Maud hauls off and shoots anyway.

" 'ARRRGH!' we hear, and a man comes racing through the trees to us. Maud has grazed his shoulder, and there's blood dripping out of his shirt.

" 'EIGHTY-TWO!' yells Maud.

" 'Eighty-two *what?*' shrieks John in exasperation, *'Maud,* that's the *mailman!* You shot Mr. Henderson, the *mailman.'*

" 'For God's sake, Maudie, put the gun down!' says Mr. Henderson.

" 'Well, Hank, fancy meeting you here,' says Maud. 'Just out bagging a few cougars. Say, is that blood on your arm? Better get home and have Lillian put a compress on that.'

"Mr. Henderson, who hasn't been mortally wounded, only scraped, goes off clutching his shoulder and muttering. By this time Edward and John and I aren't afraid of cougars, but we're simply terrified of Maud. We're worried that if we turn around and run home she'll shoot us, screaming, 'EIGHTY-THREE! EIGHTY-FOUR! EIGHTY-FIVE!'

"Edward mutters, 'I'm amazed she's only up to eighty after all these years.'

"Maud doesn't hear him because she's busy singing, 'Goin' on a cougar hunt, haroo-haroo,' with breaks now and then to bring down birds, tree branches, chipmunks, and sleeping raccoons. She's got the count up to ninety when she decides to call it quits and we head back, whistling through the woods.

" 'We bagged a few today, didn't we, kids?' she says. 'Won't you come in for some eggs?'

"We say no thank you and head on home."

Aunt Sally stood up and stretched. "And that's the end of the story."

"I think after that I'd never step into the woods again," said Amanda.

Aunt Sally smiled and looked off a long way, "Oh, yes you would, Amanda. Someday you must come and visit me. You have no idea how beautiful those woods are. How large the stillness. Like a great peacefulness extending over the land. Now, who's for some ice cream?"

FAT LITTLE MEAN GIRL!

At bedtime, as Aunt Sally tucked in Pee Wee, and Amanda and Melissa hung around the door, Pee Wee said, "Tell us the rest of the stories from the picture."

"But, Frank, I've told you all the stories," said Aunt Sally, smoothing his covers.

"Huh-uh," said Pee Wee. "You haven't told us the story of Fat Little Mean Girl."

"Yeah, that's right," said Melissa, coming in and sitting on the floor.

"Tell us now," said Amanda, joining her.

"But it's Frank's bedtime," said Aunt Sally. "And tomorrow is a busy day. Your parents get home and you have school. You all need your sleep."

"You have to tell us now," said Melissa. "Because tomorrow you leave."

"Please," said Amanda.

"Please," said Frank.

"All right," said Aunt Sally.

"And put a bear in the story, too," said Pee Wee.

"I don't put things in my stories," said Aunt Sally. "I tell you the facts, the bare facts, the whole facts, and nothing but the facts. Fat Little Mean Girl lived a short hike from us. Her father was a manager at the mill. Fat Little Mean Girl and Lyla were in the same class, and Fat Little Mean Girl would come over to our house, hoping to play with Lyla, and Lyla generally would if she wasn't busy. But if she was busy, Grandma Evelyn used to try to make me and the boys play with her. We couldn't stand her, and, as I'm sure you know, there's nothing like being made to play with someone to make you despise them all the more.

"Sometimes Fat Little Mean Girl's mother would walk her over. Her mother was roughly the size of a football stadium herself, and there must have been some deep dark secret about her because John and Edward and I would frequently catch Aunt Hattie and Grandma Evelyn whispering about her after she had left. Now that it's too late, I wish I had asked Grandma Evelyn what the deep dark secret was. She might not have told me when I was a child, but certainly when I was grownup she would have. So let that be a lesson to you, ask your parents all these questions before it's too late, and what they won't tell you about your family, I will. Anyhow, occasionally I would get dragged over to Fat Little Mean Girl's house to play with her and Lyla. Because she was so mean, she was generally awful to me once I got there and would go off with Lyla and leave me alone in her room. She had a huge room and it was just full of every conceivable prop for playing: toy stove, toy sink, shelves of dolls and doll clothes, tea sets, plastic pots and pans, train sets, blocks—the room spilled over with toys. It made me very uneasy. It made me think there must be something terribly wrong going on in a house where the grownups felt they had to cater to a child so extravagantly. I also didn't like being left alone in this room of toys, but of course Grandma Evelyn made me go when I was invited. I never knew why Fat Little Mean Girl didn't just invite Lyla and leave me alone.

"This is how things went for a couple of years. She was like a mosquito in the bedroom at night. Just when you think it's found its way out, you hear its annoying buzz. Then, for some fat little mean reason of her own, Fat Little Mean Girl decided that she didn't want Lyla to play with her anymore and she didn't want anyone else to play with Lyla, either. She was discovering that, as the daughter of a mill manager, she might be little and fat but she had power she hadn't even begun to tap. First, she began to distribute small, useless toys and hard candy to all the girls in her class except Lyla. Then she announced that there would be no more small, useless gifts to any girl who played with Lyla. This left Lyla completely in the cold. Most of the mill families were like ours and didn't see store-bought toys and treats except perhaps on Christmas or a birthday. Lyla was never so unpopular or lonely in her life. No one spoke to her, no one ate lunch with her; everyone crowded around Fat Little Mean Girl instead, to see what she had brought with her in her book bag. Lyla was never any good at fighting back. She became quieter and quieter. We all felt sorry for her. John, who had the softest spot for her, came up with an idea. One Saturday he suggested to Edward and me that we go to see the Wiccas."

"What are those?" asked Pee Wee.

"Witches," said Aunt Sally.

"No such thing," said Melissa.

"Not broomstick-flying witches. It's a kind of an alternate religion, you might say. All those islands off the coast of Canada attract people who want to fall off the earth and into a more interesting present. We had witches and other strange groups meeting all over the place on the ocean shores. John was in school with a boy named Trevor whose mother was a witch, which is how he got the idea. A lot of ladies in town weren't too nice to the witches. Some because they thought it was a lot of self-aggrandizing nonsense, and others because they thought they were agents of the devil. John suggested that we ask Trevor to take us to his mother's next meeting, and we could ask for a spell to put on Fat Little Mean Girl. Trevor agreed, on the condition that we wouldn't show ourselves until he had time to get home, because his mother scared him to death. The witches claimed to be some kind of ultrafeminist group in tune with nature and the moon and stuff, but Trevor's mother was a real terror. I had seen her shake Trevor until his teeth rattled, right on Main Street. At the next full moon, Trevor led us to the spit of land going out into the ocean where the Wiccas had a bonfire. We promised Trevor that they could torture us with dehydrated catgut and we'd never tell them that he had led us there."

"Did they use dehydrated catgut?" asked Amanda.

"Trevor had told us that they planned to sell it door-to-door like Girl Scout cookies. All these local groups were big on fund-raising. Of course, no one ever knocked on our door and tried to sell us anything like that, but we were off the beaten track. Anyhow, there they all stood in their long black robes with crescent moons and strange lettering painted on them. We stayed hidden in the bushes, watching them chanting around the fire and throwing colored powders into it.

"Edward whispered, 'If they're so in tune with the natural world, how come they don't know we're hiding in the bushes?'

"Then I sneezed. I'll never forget that. And they all turned and *ran* at us. Well, it's one thing to spy on a bunch of witches and it's another to be charged by them. We fell over each other trying to get out of that bush. John tripped and as we helped him up the witches descended on us.

"Trevor's mother recognized us and said in an ordinary, crabby voice, 'Well, Edward, John, and Sally. What in hell are you doing here?'

"I had expected her to speak in Wicca, I guess, but she just sounded like your basic annoyed mom, except none of the moms we knew swore.

" 'We have come for a spell,' said John.

" 'To put on Fat Little Mean Girl,' said Edward.

"I nudged him, because most grownups would say not to be rude, but the Wiccas just regarded us, considering.

" 'What do you want to do to her exactly?' asked Trevor's mom.

" 'Well, we don't want to kill her,' I said, narrowing down the possibilities.

" 'Oh, for heaven's sake, don't waste my time,' said Trevor's mom. 'What do you think we are, the Mafia?'

" 'We only do spells of kindness,' said another Wicca.

" 'Well, that won't do us any good,' I said, 'because she's torturing my sister and leaving her to a life of loneliness and we want to make her stop.'

" 'Why not *try* a little kindness?' asked one of the Wiccas.

" 'It'll cost you nine dollars and ninety-nine cents. Plus tax,' said Trevor's mom, who was awfully businesslike for someone who, not ten minutes before, had been dancing around the moon.

" 'We don't have that kind of money,' I said.

" 'We don't even have the tax,' said John.

" 'Then scram,' said Trevor's mom.

" 'Couldn't we just hang out and watch you do a few spells?' asked Edward.

" 'This isn't the circus,' said Trevor's mom, giving us such a truly witchy look that we turned and ran all the way home.

" 'Nine dollars and ninety-nine cents plus tax,' said Edward, as we panted by our door. 'What are they, nuts?' Which I thought was certainly belaboring the obvious. 'Where are we going to get that kind of dough?'

"Fortunately, a way immediately presented itself to us. The next night after dinner, Robbie was in the living room, drawing with the pencils Great-uncle Louis had given him, while we all sat around and gnawed our sticks.

" 'What's that a picture of, Robbie, boy?' asked Great-uncle Louis.

"Robbie held up his picture, and Great-uncle Louis said, 'Evelyn, I think that boy has talent!'

" 'Yes, of course he has talent, Louis,' said Grandma Evelyn. She was always very polite, but as the years went on, she began to lose it with Great-uncle Louis.

" 'And talent should be rewarded. Robbie, get me my wallet from my bureau.'

"Robbie got the wallet while Edward and John and I watched bug-eyed. He took a whole dollar out and gave it to Robbie, who beamed and went back to drawing.

" 'Louis, can I speak to you for a moment?' said Grandma Evelyn, and she led Great-uncle Louis out of the room. I don't know what she said to him, whether it was something about not singling Robbie out so much, or not giving us children money, but Great-uncle Louis never did that again *in public*. Robbie was more than happy to tell us that privately Great-uncle Louis slipped him a buck on a regular basis. It became quite obvious what the solution to our financial crisis was going to be."

"You took Daddy's money?" said Melissa.

"Exactly. Robbie kept his money all over his room. There were dollars in old pants pockets and dollars on his bookshelf and dollars lying around, dust-covered. We just nipped in every other day or so until we had eleven dollars, which we figured would cover the nine dollars and ninety-nine cents plus tax. None of us were sure how much tax there was on nine dollars and ninety-nine cents."

"Didn't he miss it?" asked Amanda.

"Yes, he did. Or he thought he did. But he was so careless, and Great-uncle Louis was always providing him with more, that he was never sure if he was really missing his money. We thought we were teaching him a valuable lesson about taking care of his things. He was trying to save up for a pony, so we figured we were also teaching him about realistic expectations."

"Like we try to improve Pee Wee," said Melissa.

"Precisely," said Aunt Sally, but Melissa thought she gave

her a funny look. It wasn't at all sympathetic. "When we had our eleven dollars we asked Trevor when the next Wicca meeting was. It turned out they met at full moon, so we waited for the next one and went down to the ocean. We gave them the eleven dollars, and they gave us a vial of red powder.

" 'Do we get any change?' I asked.

" 'What is this, Meyer's Cash and Carry?' asked Trevor's mom. 'Now listen, this powder should make this kid less mean, but you have to spread it on some food. Got that? She's got to take it with food. It's fairly acidic, and we don't want her getting an ulcer, right?'

" 'Oh, right,' said Edward.

" 'Definitely,' said John.

" 'Get outta here,' said Trevor's mom, and believe me, we did.

"The next day we put some red powder on our lunchtime chocolate-chip cookies. It was the ultimate sacrifice, but we had to save Lyla. Then we gave the cookies to Fat Little Mean Girl, who was so mean she didn't even say thank you but just scarfed them down. We waited to see if she would turn nice, but she didn't. She was just as fat and mean as always.

" 'Now what do we do?' I whispered to Edward.

" 'There's nothing for it but to give her the rest of our lunch, too,' said Edward. 'She's obviously so mean that she needs a bigger dosage. A huge dosage.'

" 'But can we get her to eat all that?' asked John.

" 'We have to try,' I said desperately.

"We took our sandwiches and apples and dusted them with the red powder and offered them to Fat Little Mean Girl. Well, she wasn't called Fat Little Mean Girl for nothing. She inhaled that food like dust up a vacuum, but it didn't make her any nicer. She was just as fat and mean as ever. So we took up a collection. We got people to give us discarded crackers and cheese, chips, candy. Edward went about saying, 'Alms for the poor, alms for the poor.' John sprinkled powder on the food and Fat Little Mean Girl ate it. It was incredible. Whatever you gave her, she unquestioningly consumed. It got to be kind of fascinating after a while. But she wasn't getting any nicer and we were getting desperate. Lunchtime was almost over. Just as the bell rang and we started to walk defeatedly up the playground hill to the school door, Fat Little Mean Girl leaned over and threw up. She threw up all over her shoes and her dress and her stockings. When the teacher saw her, she said, 'My goodness, are you sick, dear?'

" 'No,' said Fat Little Mean Girl, pointing to us. 'It's all their fault. They gave me too much to eat.'

" 'You can lead a horse to water but you can't make it drink,' said the teacher as we all stood in the schoolyard looking at the mess. 'I think you had better go home and change before you come back in the school.'

"Fat Little Mean Girl went home and told her mother that the teacher had called her a horse. First Fat Little Mean Girl's mother tried to have the teacher fired, and then finally she put Fat Little Mean Girl in a private school way up in Duncan, and we never had to play with her again. Lyla never knew what we did for her, which was just as well, because I don't think she would have approved of our methods."

"But was it the spell that made her throw up, do you think?" asked Melissa.

"Lord, no, the kid ate everything in sight, and who knows what that powder really was. Nothing poisonous, as there were no lasting effects, but more than likely it was a scam by these ladies, or just wishful thinking. Hoping they had extra powers and coming to believe after a while they really did. John wanted to get our money back, because, as he pointed out, Fat Little Mean Girl never did become nice, which is what they *said* would happen. However, as all ended well, we finally decided to leave it alone."

"I almost feel sorry for Fat Little Mean Girl," said Amanda.

"Why?" asked Melissa. "She was a terrible person."

"I know, but throwing up in public is so embarrassing," said Amanda.

"She got her revenge," said Aunt Sally grimly.

"How?" asked Pee Wee. "Did she put red powder in your food?"

"No, worse. She grew up and married your Uncle Edward," said Aunt Sally.

"NO!" shouted Melissa. "Is that Aunt Marianne who was drowned at sea with Uncle Edward on their honeymoon?"

"That's the one. That's why she's in the picture, otherwise I would just as soon have forgotten her, but she loomed large, although not long, as it turned out." Aunt Sally looked at the picture and sighed. "I ought to do you a nicer one than this pencil sketch. I'll get my paints out when I get home and do another one and send it to you for Christmas."

"But you won't leave anyone out, will you?" asked Amanda, studying the picture.

"No," said Aunt Sally. "I won't leave anyone out."

THE TROLLS!

When Pee Wee was asleep, Aunt Sally came into the girls' room to say good night.

"Tonight you have to finish the story of the trolls," said Amanda.

"But it's lights-out time already," said Aunt Sally.

"Then turn off the light and tell us in the dark," said Melissa.

Aunt Sally snapped off the light and heaved a small sigh so faint it barely rustled the dark. Then she sat down creakily in the rocking chair and rocked silently until the girls began to wonder if she was going to tell them the story or not.

As if reading their thoughts, she said, "I'm just trying to remember this right . . . which is hard to do with memories that hurt. Your mind skirts around the details. It was Halloween and Robbie was in grade four. It had been a whole year since he won the poster contest. We had gotten our report cards. I always did just fine on mine, seldom getting less than an A, except in handwriting. This was Robbie's first year of letter grades. He got mostly B's, but he got an A in art. That wouldn't have been so terrible, but when I opened my report card, I got a B in art. I had a new teacher and she obviously didn't appreciate my innate talent. She wrote that I worked too quickly and should slow down and try to finish things more carefully. Of course, now that I'm grown up, I realize that she was simply a color-in-the-lines type teacher and it meant nothing, but then it was a dreadful blow to my ego. Especially since art was considered an easy A, like music. How could one fail in art? And, to me, a B was a miserable failure. Because Robbie's only A was in art, he made a great deal of it, and so did Great-uncle Louis. I had almost forgotten the whole poster-contest business, but here it was—a fresh humiliation. Deep inside of me, twisting and turning like a worm, was the thought of the trolls.

"On Halloween night, Edward, John, and I planned to go to the beach and see if anyone was setting off fireworks there and, if not, head into town. We hadn't planned to take Robbie, who usually went trick-or-treating with Grandpa Willie, but this year Grandma Evelyn decided he was old enough to go with us.

" 'I don't want to go to the beach,' he whined as we set off. 'I want to go to town and trick-or-treat.'

" 'You have to go to the beach because Mom says you have to stay with us and that's where we're going,' said John shortly.

" 'I'm not going to,' said Robbie, heading in the direction of town. We trailed behind him because we knew that once Robbie's mind was made up there was no point in trying to dissuade him.

" 'The little stinker,' said John. 'I suppose by the time we do get back to the beach all the fireworks will be over.'

" 'I knew he'd ruin Halloween,' said Edward. 'Great-uncle Louis has completely spoiled him.'

" 'Great-uncle Louis has turned him into a monster,' I said. 'What he needs is a good scare. Think of it, suppose there are such things as trolls? We leave Robbie on the beach as bait and we grab him before the trolls can get him. He gets a good scare and we get to see the trolls. That's more spectacular than fireworks.'

" 'I don't believe in trolls,' said John.

" 'It works either way. If there are trolls, we rescue him; if there aren't, he still gets scared,' I said.

" 'I don't like it,' said John.

" 'Because *you're* scared?' I asked. 'What about our test of courage? What about Maud and the cougars?'

" 'All Maud and the cougars proved was that in a scary situation the three of us together haven't got enough spit left to lick an envelope. We'd probably see the trolls and fall dead from heart attacks,' said John.

" 'But you don't believe in the trolls,' I said.

" 'Hurry up!' yelled Robbie, who was still marching ahead of us. We followed him limply around town, trick-or-treating. We could hear the sound of fireworks going off everywhere and knew that soon they would be finished, just as the trick-or-treating trickled to a few older children like ourselves.

" 'I'm tired. I want to go home now,' Robbie announced. He had led the way the whole time, with the three of us ignominiously following in his footsteps. We could hear fireworks going off in the park.

" 'Let's just go check out those fireworks,' said Edward.

" 'No, I want to go home. I don't like fireworks,' said Robbie.

" 'Listen, we followed *you*, the least you can do is go to the park for ten minutes for us,' said John.

" 'I'm tired and I want to go home,' said Robbie. He charged ahead. John wanted to grab his arm and drag him back to the park, but every time we tried to catch up, Robbie ran ahead. Finally, the sound of whizzing and banging ceased and we knew it was over for another year.

" 'Thanks a lot, Robbie!' called John.

"Edward had been suspiciously silent through all this. Now he called, 'Robbie, I'll give you all my chocolate bars if you go down to the beach with us.'

"Robbie stopped and turned around. 'And then we'd go right home?'

" 'Yes, if there are no fireworks,' said Edward.

" 'If I have to stay and watch fireworks, I want all of John's chocolate bars, too,' said Robbie.

" 'No,' said John.

" 'You can have all mine,' I said quickly.

" 'Well, all right,' said Robbie, and let us catch up to him. We walked down the path to the beach. The tide was changing and the waves were crashing in. It was a dark night, with only a thin sliver of moon and a misty rain beginning to fall. The wind down by the ocean whistled loudly through the trees.

" 'There's no one down here!' yelled Robbie, over the sound of the waves. 'I want to go home!'

" 'There *is* someone down here!' I yelled back, yanking at John's and Edward's sleeves, indicating that it was time to make our move. 'There's the trolls, Robbie!' The three of us turned around and ran up the path as far as the gravestones. Then we stopped and giggled, expecting to hear Robbie crying and calling from the beach, but the beach was eerily silent except for the roar of the waves.

" 'Aw, we ought to go get him,' said John. 'He just acts that way because he hates being the littlest. This is mean.'

" 'Yeah, all right,' said Edward. 'But I still think it served him right.'

"We started walking back down to where we had left him. I felt a kind of delicious freedom, as though this twisting and turning worm I had harbored for so many months had finally been released. I knew a mean act shouldn't make one feel so good, but it was completely liberating, like being let out of a plastic bag and allowed to breathe again. It was with a lighthearted step that I approached the rocks where we left him, but when we got there, he was gone.

" 'That little jerk,' muttered Edward. 'Robbie, come out! It's time to go home!'

"He still didn't appear.

" 'This isn't funny!' I called. 'Mom's going to be mad if we don't get home soon!'

" 'Come on! We're sorry. You can have my chocolate bars, too!' yelled John. We stood there for some minutes yelling, until it occurred to us that Robbie really wasn't there. We clung to each other, and I realized that if I was too terrified to be alone on the beach, Robbie must have run home immediately.

" 'Oh, this is great!' said John. 'If he's wandered into the bush, he could be lost entirely.'

" 'But he knows the paths home,' I said. 'He wouldn't be so stupid as to go off the paths, would he?'

" 'I don't know; we better get Mom,' said John, and he began to run back up from the beach. I volunteered shakily to stay rooted on Caroline's and Frank's gravestones and continue to call Robbie's name in case he wandered close enough to hear it. Edward and John ran home. I had never really believed in the trolls, but as I sat there in the cold, niggling at the back of my mind was the thought of hulking forms shambling along the beach and taking Robbie away forever. It had been what I had wanted. I had simply wanted Robbie gone. Now he was.

"Soon Grandpa Willie and Uncle Louis came down. Grandma Evelyn was in the house waiting for the Royal Canadian Mounted Police. John and Edward and I were sent home, and when the RCMP arrived, they organized search parties. We saw lights in the woods for the next two hours, and finally Great-uncle Louis found him and brought him home. Grandma Evelyn put Robbie to bed. Edward and John and I hung around nervously, waiting for someone to yell at us when Robbie spilled the beans about what we had done, but Robbie didn't say a word, which was most unlike him. Grandma Evelyn and Grandpa Willie served sandwiches and coffee to the search parties and at last everyone went home and we all went to bed.

"The next morning, when we compared notes, Great-uncle Louis said he had found Robbie being carried off by the trolls, and as soon as they put him down and turned their backs, he had scooped him up and run off with him, with the heavy-footed thud of the trolls' feet behind. Grandma Evelyn said that wasn't amusing. That Great-uncle Louis was either delusional or heartless, and she sent him packing. She said it had been the worst scare of her life, and she had no patience with anyone who could tell her such a thing. We never saw Great-uncle Louis again. Robbie never told Grandma or Grandpa that we had left him on the beach for the trolls. Perhaps because Grandma Evelyn had had such a violent reaction to the mention of trolls, but I think because we frightened him. John later confessed to Lyla because he couldn't stand the guilt, I guess, and even though Lyla couldn't seem to believe that we would do such a thing, after that she and I could never be close. John and Edward and I tried explaining to Robbie that it was only a Halloween joke. That we would never let the trolls get him. Robbie seemed to accept our apology, but I guess knowing that your own trusted family could give you away, even in jest, well, it changes things. It changes things forever. If we wanted to cure him of his self-centered ways, we certainly had. He was never boastful or mean with us again. He wasn't, in the end, ever with us again."

"But were there trolls? Did he tell you that the trolls took him, like Great-uncle Louis said?" asked Amanda.

"Yeah, what did Daddy say happened?" asked Melissa.

"He didn't tell us anything," said Aunt Sally.

"But it couldn't have been trolls," said Melissa. "Because Great-uncle Louis said that once you give something to the trolls you can never ever have it back."

"But we never did get Robbie back. Or Lyla. Or Great-uncle Louis. We thought we would be well rid of him, but a lot of life was gone from the dinner table after he left. We all drifted apart, until finally we grew up and John went to Alaska, Lyla and Robbie went to college in Ohio and settled here and we rarely saw them, Edward drowned at sea, and Grandma and Grandpa died. Now there's just me on the island and there is no more family. So either Great-uncle Louis was right and the trolls never do give back what they take, or some acts alter everything forever, but that's how it was on the island. And when I pass our old clapboard house that I loved so much, I am a stranger. Now listen, it's very late. That's the end of my stories. I'll see you in the morning." Aunt Sally stood up and walked quietly out, closing the door behind her.

"Wow," said Melissa softly.

"It wasn't frightening like I thought it would be," said Amanda.

"No," said Melissa. "It was just sad."

Merry Christmas!

The next day, the children ran home from school. Their parents had arrived in the afternoon and met them at the door, full of hugs and kisses and presents. There was lots of excited chatter all through dinner, and then it was time to take Aunt Sally to the airport.

"He never looks at her," whispered Melissa to Amanda when they were getting on their coats to go to the airport.

"I know," said Amanda. "He talks to her, and he doesn't seem mad and stuff, but he looks at her feet."

"Or over her shoulder."

"And he threw out that picture she made of the family. Did you notice that? When we were opening presents in the living room, he kind of swept it up with the packing paper."

"Why didn't you stop him?" asked Melissa.

"Because he ripped it up as he stuffed things in a garbage bag. Anyhow, she promised to send us a better one at Christmas. Doesn't it seem strange to think that Daddy and Robbie in the stories are the same?"

"Girls, come on!" called their mother from the driveway.

They grabbed their coats and joined Aunt Sally in the back of the van.

"You have to visit again soon, doesn't she, Daddy?" said Melissa, holding Aunt Sally's arm.

"Um-hmm," mumbled their father, backing out of the driveway.

"Or perhaps our next family vacation will be to Vancouver Island," said the children's mother. "Wouldn't that be nice, Robbie?"

"Doris, see if you can wipe off the inside of the windshield, it's fogging up again," said their father, passing her a Kleenex.

At the airport, goodbyes were said, and the ride home was unusually quiet.

"It was a cool tree house she built me," said Pee Wee.

"And nobody could eat a bean like her," said Amanda.

"Daddy, were there really trolls on Vancouver Island?" asked Melissa.

"What trolls?" said their father. "Doris, did you unpack my gray sweater? I haven't seen it since I've been home."

Later, in bed, Melissa said, "Well, he didn't say there weren't trolls."

"How much of those stories do you believe? She made them seem so real when she was here, but they couldn't actually have gnawed on sticks, could they?"

"I can't get the mysterious man out of my head," said Amanda. "What if he's still alive somewhere?"

"She never said if Aunt Hattie was dead. Maybe they are in some nursing home together."

"No, I'm pretty sure she did say Aunt Hattie was dead."

"Do you think her gravestone is on the path by Caroline's and Frank's? That would be so neat."

"Do you know where I think the mysterious man is?"

"Where?"

"With Elvis."

The next two months were busy, ordinary months, with school and violin and soccer, and Aunt Sally's stories began to seem far away. Then it was Christmas vacation. The day before Christmas, a package arrived from Vancouver Island.

"Well, my lands," said their mother. "What is this? From Aunt Sally to you children. Isn't that nice?"

The children crowded around her and opened it. It was a large framed painting, exactly the same as the sketch she had done. She hadn't left anyone out and, in fact, had added something.

"Hey!" said Pee Wee. "Look, she put us in the picture."

There the three of them stood, at the top of the hill overlooking the ocean, wearing their Halloween costumes. Melissa was dressed in her ruffled stepmother dress, Amanda was in the velvet stepsister dress, and Pee Wee was dressed as a ghost.

Melissa turned to Amanda and said, "How did she know?"

Go Fish!

GO FISH

POLLY HORVATH

What did you want to be when you grew up?
I wanted to be a writer, a dancer, and a nun.

What was your worst subject in school?
Math. When I got to geometry in tenth grade, it made me weep.

Where do you write your books?
I have an office in our basement. It's very private with a window overlooking a lot of fruit trees where the horse likes to graze. He snorts, I write. Sometimes, I snort. I don't know if he writes.

Which of your characters is most like you?
Uncle Martin in *The Corps of the Bare-Boned Plane*.

Are you a morning person or a night owl?
I'm a morning person. When I'm doing a first draft, I have to work in the morning.

What's your idea of the best meal ever?
Cheese and crackers, and red wine. Or lobster and clams at a lobster pound in Maine. Or a cruiser day lunch, which only people who have gone to Camp Nebagamon will understand.

Which do you like better: cats or dogs?
Dogs. I love dogs. I could never live without a dog.

What do you value most in your friends?
Tolerance and finding the same things funny that I do.

Where do you go for peace and quiet?
We live in miles of wilderness on our doorstep, so generally, I just go outdoors.

What's your favorite song?
"Hallelujah" by Leonard Cohen, sung by Rufus Wainwright.

Who is your favorite fictional character?
Jo March or anyone from *Sweet Thursday* by John Steinbeck, which is my favorite book.

What are you most afraid of?
Something happening to the people I love.

What time of the year do you like best?
Autumn, around Halloween, when everything is golden.

If you were stranded on a desert island, who would you want for company?
My husband, daughters, our dog, and our horse. Then, I wouldn't be stranded.

Keep reading for an excerpt from Polly Horvath's
The Pepins and Their Problems,
available now in paperback from Square Fish.

EXCERPT

There are always problems in the lives of Mr. and Mrs. Pepin; their children, Petunia and Irving; their dog, Roy; their cat, Miranda; and their very fine neighbor Mr. Bradshaw. Now, all families have problems, and all families, one hopes, eventually solve them, but the Pepins and their very fine neighbor Mr. Bradshaw have problems of such a bizarre nature that they are never able to find a solution and get on with their lives without the help of you, dear reader.

Just recently the Pepins awoke to find toads in their shoes. This was quite a puzzler.

"What shall we do?" asked Mrs. Pepin, who needed to put her shoes on so she could catch the 8:05 train to her part-time job at the Domestic Laboratory, on the outskirts of beautiful downtown Peony, where she led the field in peanut butter experiments. The Domestic Laboratory was not a strict company, but it did require its workers to arrive shod.

"What shall we do?" asked Mr. Pepin, who needed his shoes so he could drive them both to the train station. There he would catch the 8:10 to work at the cardboard factory, where he was in charge of corrugation.

"I am not putting my foot in a toad-filled shoe," said Petunia, who was in the fifth grade, where she wasn't in charge of anything.

"Maybe we should go next door and ask Mr. Bradshaw if he has toads in his shoes," said Irving, who was a sixth-grade genius and in charge of leading all charges.

In the end, that is what the Pepins did. They went next door to their very fine neighbor Mr. Bradshaw, who was eating corn twinklies and hadn't looked at his shoes yet. The Pepins explained to Mr. Bradshaw what the problem was, and together they went to examine Mr. Bradshaw's very fine shoes. There were toads in every single pair. Even in the galoshes.

"Thank you for calling this to my attention,"

said Mr. Bradshaw, and then, because he was an exemplary host as well as a very fine neighbor, he poured bowls of corn twinklies all round.

The Pepins and Mr. Bradshaw could not imagine what to do with their toad-filled shoes. How had the toads gotten into all the shoes, and how were the Pepins to get them out? They thought for a very long while, but even Irving the genius was unable to think of a solution.

This is where I must ask for your assistance, dear reader. Many, many books are written to be read passively. The author discourages reader input. The author actively dislikes it. Shoo, shoo, says the author to his pesky readers. But then most books, one could almost say all others, are not written about the Pepins, and therefore the characters do not need help. Or if they need it, the characters seem to think they must persevere on their own with silent dignity. Not so the Pepins. The Pepins love help in solving their problems, by which they mean having others aid them in their endless speculations. Could this be? Could that be? How does one get down off a duck? Or get toads out of one's shoes?

Fortunately, this author is endowed with unusually large psychic antennae. She is deeply attuned to her readers. If you put one finger on

each temple and concentrate, she will be able to hear your solution and share it with the Pepins and other readers. No other author on the face of the earth is able to do this. Do not expect it of them.

So go ahead, think your solutions very hard, think them northward because your author lives, most likely, above you. No, not in heaven, angelic though she is, but in Canada. Although to hear some Canadians, you'd think the two were interchangeable. Just do not get carried away and shout them out loud if your parents are asleep, because it is past your bedtime and you are reading this book under your covers by flashlight. I, your author, do not wish to get in trouble.

Wait! I hear readers!

As usual, explanations come more easily than solutions. Our readers are rife with explanations, but I do not hear any solutions per se. That is fine. I welcome all input: solutions, explanations, answers, questions, speculations. A writer's life is a lonely one.

A reader from Tinton Falls, New Jersey, thinks an ecological problem has caused a sudden growth in the toad population, although a reader from Lake Nebagamon, Wisconsin, asks why the toads have taken to shoes.

A reader from Normal, Illinois, thinks Irving

has secretly filled the shoes with toads. I'm afraid this idea must be disregarded, as Irving, apart from being a genius, is a model citizen. But we can certainly see what kinds of tricks some of our readers would be up to if not carefully watched.

A reader from Wiggonsville, Ohio, thinks that aliens from space had put tadpoles in the shoes, and the toads had *grown* there. I'm afraid that readers from Pottsville, Pennsylvania; Vinton, Iowa; Miami, Oklahoma (please stop shouting that Miami is in Florida. There is *too* a Miami, Oklahoma. If you don't believe me, get out your atlas)—anyway, I'm afraid that all these readers also insist that the aliens have been at it, and to them I say, and listen closely because I am only going to say this once, *nobody*, not even an alien, has *that* much time.

The correct answer comes from a dear reader in Kalamazoo, Michigan, who suggests that the toads have merely run out of toadstools to sit on and are hiding in shoes until more toadstools are made ready. Once the Pepins and their very fine neighbor Mr. Bradshaw were apprised of this, they ran (barefoot) to the nearest woods and found toadstools to lure the toads out of their shoes. Everyone was late for work and school, but at least they arrived shod.

A day that begins with toads in the shoes is a long one. The Pepins were tired that evening, and so was their very fine neighbor Mr. Bradshaw. All were ready to retire to bed early when Petunia, who had a keen aesthetic sense (meaning she sometimes saw pretty things even where no pretty things existed), noticed the beginning of a magnificent sunset.

"Mom, Dad, Irving, Miranda, Roy," she called, "this small picture window doesn't do the night sky justice. Let us all climb up on the roof to see the whole horizon. Roy, go next door and fetch Mr. Bradshaw."

Roy went next door immediately. The Pepins, when they were teaching Roy to sit and stay, also taught him the go-next-door-and-fetch-Mr.-Bradshaw command. Mr. Bradshaw came over at once and helped the Pepins put a ladder against the side of the house. Everyone climbed up to the roof. Irving carried Roy, and Petunia carried Miranda. Mr. Pepin carried Mrs. Pepin, even though she did not particularly want to be carried, but just to round things out. Mr. Bradshaw, who had no one to carry, stole a squirrel. Mr. and Mrs. Pepin were the last ones up, and after Mr. Pepin put Mrs. Pepin down, he turned around to look at the sunset and accidentally kicked the ladder, which fell all the way to the ground with a great *clunk*. The Pepins and Mr. Bradshaw were stuck on the roof. Of course, they could think of no way down.

"What a thing to happen," said Mrs. Pepin, "on a day that began with toads in our shoes."

As it became evident that they were not going to get off the roof that night, Mrs. Pepin turned to her very fine neighbor and said, "Dear Mr. Bradshaw, I had always hoped that if we were someday fortunate enough to have you as our houseguest, we would at least be able to serve you a little cheese. Nevertheless, won't you be our roofguest tonight?"

"Dear lady," replied Mr. Bradshaw, "I do not see that I have a choice."

Or does he? Put your fingers to your temples, dear reader, and please help me solve this Pepin problem.